Chrissy grabbed Brett's hand and slithered off the surfboard into his arms. She fought to regain her balance, flinging her arms around his neck as the wave threatened to sweep her on with it. As she stood up, Brett tightened his arms around her waist.

Chrissy gave an embarrassed smile and glanced back at the shore. Someone was standing a few feet away, watching her intently. As her eyes met his, she saw recognition spread across his face.

"It *is* you, Chrissy," Jeff said. "I thought I was seeing a mirage."

"Hi, Jeff," she began, conscious that Brett was still holding her. "I was just taking my first surfing lesson. . ."

Just at that moment Tod came riding effortlessly in on the next wave. "Hey, Brett!" he yelled. "Get your hands off her! She's mine!"

Jeff's eyes narrowed. He glanced up at Tod, at Brett, and then back to Chrissy. "Well, good seeing you, Chrissy," he said sharply. "I don't want to keep you from your surfing lesson!"

Then he turned and walked back up the beach, disappearing into the crowd before Chrissy could break free from Brett's embrace.

Other books in the **SUGAR & SPICE** series:

1 Two Girls, One Boy
2 Trading Places
3 The Last Dance
4 Dear Cousin
5 Nothing in Common
6 Flip Side
7 Tug of War

COMING SOON

9 Double Take
#10 Make Me a Star

Janet
Quin-Harkin's

Sugar & Spice

Surf's Up!

IVY BOOKS • NEW YORK

Ivy Books
Published by Ballantine Books
Copyright © 1987 by Butterfield Press, Inc. & Janet Quin-Harkin

Produced by Butterfield Press, Inc.
133 Fifth Avenue
New York, New York 10003

Library of Congress Catalog Card Number: 87-91524

ISBN 0-8041-0063-2

Manufactured in the United States of America

First Edition: December 1987

SURF'S UP!

Janet Quin-Harkin

Chapter 1

"Come on, Chrissy, you can make it. Only one more hill and you're home," Chrissy Madden told herself as she jogged the last stretch of the way back to the apartment house. Her legs were aching and she was breathing heavily, but she forced herself to keep going.

Right foot, left foot, right foot, left foot, she kept repeating in her mind. *Boy, I hope this is worth it,* she thought. *I can't go back to Danbury looking like one of the Masterson's hogs. I'd never hear the end of it—especially from those bratty brothers of mine.*

At the thought of her brothers' teasing, Chrissy pushed herself faster up the hill. Her long blonde ponytail swung back and forth with each step, and she could feel the sweat trickling down the sides of her face.

Funny, I don't remember the hill being this long or this steep, Chrissy thought, wiping the perspiration onto the back of her hand. Up ahead she spotted a group of three guys walking toward her. *Hmmm, not bad*, she thought as she sucked in her stomach. *Of course, none of them are nearly as gorgeous as Jeff. . . .* Chrissy smiled as a picture of her boyfriend flashed through her mind.

"Hey, babe, what's the hurry?" one of the guys called out, breaking into Chrissy's reverie. She grinned at him and ran past.

As she neared the top of the hill, Chrissy slowed her pace down to a brisk walk. She stopped outside the big wooden house where for the past year she'd been living with her cousin Caroline and her Aunt Edith and Uncle Richard in the third-floor apartment. Soon, however, she'd be going home—back to good old Danbury, Iowa.

Chrissy turned around to look back down the hill toward the glittering blue waters of the San Francisco Bay. *I sure will miss this view*, she thought, *and everything else about San Francisco. I can't believe I didn't want to come here at first. What a dummy I was!*

Chrissy shook her head and climbed up the stairs to the apartment.

"I'm home!" she yelled, opening the door. "I just ran two whole miles. Don't I get a medal?"

When no one answered she swung the door shut and headed toward the kitchen for a cool glass of milk. But she quickly forgot about the milk when she saw what was waiting for her on the kitchen table—a postcard from Hawaii! It had to be from Jeff!

Chrissy glanced at the picture of the sun setting over a white sand beach ringed with palm trees, then she flipped it over to read the back.

Dear Chrissy,

Hawaii is the greatest! The band's got a regular gig at the B— C— in Waikiki (Chrissy tried to make out the name of the club, but she couldn't decipher Jeff's handwriting, so she skipped it and went on), so I'm real busy, but, of course, not too busy to have fun! Hope you're enjoying your last few weeks in SF. (Chrissy had trouble with this word, too, but decided it must be "San Francisco.") Take care.

Love,
Jeff (who else?)

Chrissy read the card again, then gazed at the picture, imagining that she and Jeff were walking hand in hand along that very beach, feeling the warm sand under their feet and the gentle ocean lapping at their toes. Then they would run together into the calm, clear surf and Jeff's arm would come around her and . . .

Absolute heaven, she thought with a wistful sigh.

Jeff had been touring with his band since the beginning of the summer, and she missed his easygoing smile and twinkling blue eyes. She always had so much fun with Jeff—he made her laugh more than anyone else she'd ever known— and he was always doing exciting things. When Chrissy had seen him a few weeks ago, he had been playing in Reno, Nevada, and she and Caroline had been counselors at a nearby camp. He'd gotten a friend of his to pick them up at the camp in a limousine and drive them to Reno. How she wished she had a picture of *that* to show her friends back in Danbury!

Chrissy grinned as she shuffled through the rest of the mail. At the bottom of the pile she found a letter addressed to her in her mother's neat handwriting. She grabbed the letter and took it and the postcard to the room down the hall that she shared with Caroline.

She placed the postcard carefully on the table next to her bed and sat down. *Yuck, I feel disgusting after that jog,* she thought, slipping her sweaty feet out of her sneakers. *I know, I'll take a quick shower, then relax on the porch with Mom's letter.*

Ten minutes later Chrissy was lying on top of a beach towel on the porch wearing the tiniest of bikinis. *Won't they all envy my tan back home?* she thought with satisfaction. *At least that will make up for my extra flab. So what if I don't fit into my cheerleading uniform? Everyone will be looking at my great tan!*

Chrissy sat up and crossed her legs into a more comfortable Indian-style position, then opened her mother's letter.

My dear, dear Honeybun,

How are you? We are all fine here, and looking forward to having you back home with us. Although they won't admit it, I can tell that even your brothers can't wait to see you again. Jimmy is saving up some "knock-knock" jokes to tell you that he thinks are just the bee's knees. Tom and Will are tired of hearing them, and so are your dad and I. Ben has been coming around a lot lately, which is good for Jimmy, because Ben is the only one left who laughs at his jokes!

And speaking of Ben, he's been asking for you—

Chrissy took a deep breath, then let it out slowly. *Darn that Ben! Doesn't he know what "over" means?* she thought, scowling. *We are history, Ben*, she declared silently. *Finished.* Chrissy cringed as she read the rest of the paragraph.

He's wondering when you'll be home. Frankly, honeybun, I'm wondering, too. Not that I want to rush you back, because I can imagine what a terrific time you must be having, but just to let you know that we miss you.

And I miss you, too, Chrissy thought. Much as she loved the Kirbys, and especially having a cousin like Caroline—who was more like the sister she never had—they just weren't her family. For one thing, they didn't make nearly enough noise! And she missed the farm, too. Those three weeks she and Caroline had spent on the farm back in April had reminded her of that. Nothing in San Francisco could replace the glorious feeling of being surrounded by wide-open spaces, or the comfort of knowing everyone in town. *Yeah, Danbury's a pretty nice place,* Chrissy decided. But then she thought of leaving San Francisco, and she got a big lump in her throat. *If only I could be in both places at the same time,* she mused, *that would be perfect.*

Chrissy shook back her mane of blonde hair, feeling it tickle her bare shoulders, and continued reading.

Well, that's enough nagging from your old ma. Now tell me, what is this Jeff Dixon like? Is he really as hunky as you say?

Reading the last sentence over, Chrissy had to laugh aloud at her mother using the word "hunky." It just didn't sound right coming from her. She'd have to tell her mother that the answer was "yes, definitely!" In fact, she was waiting for Jeff to return from Hawaii so they could have a few last days together before she headed home.

Chrissy gazed down at the Bay below, and thought that Jeff's eyes were the exact same shade of blue, and they even sparkled just like the water sparkled in the sunlight. *I wonder what he's doing now?* she thought. Before she had time to think of an answer, she heard the sound of footsteps clattering up the stairs to the porch.

Chapter 2

"Chrissy, where are you? Chrissy?" Caroline's yell traveled ahead of her up the steps from the street. Chrissy looked up from her bench and grinned. It was funny how everyone used to think Caroline was so quiet. Since Chrissy had arrived in California, she had noticed her cousin becoming more outspoken and impulsive—at least Caroline had learned a *few* things from her.

"Up here!" Chrissy called back. Immediately Caroline's head appeared around the corner of the steps. Her ash-blonde hair, sun-streaked almost white in front, bounced around her face as she leaped up the steps two at a time. She broke into a delighted grin when she spied her cousin.

"Oh, there you are! I'm so glad you're home, I thought you might have been out buying even more clothes to add to the covered wagon."

"I am definitely putting a stop to my shopping sprees," Chrissy said, "or all that lovely money from camp will disappear. From now on I'm going to be sensible about money. And money I make in the future is going straight to my college fund. No more frivolous spending for me—no, sirree!"

Caroline laughed. "I can tell you've stopped spending money on clothes," she said, "because you obviously had only a couple of dollars to spend on that bikini. Poor thing, you could only afford three inches of fabric!"

Chrissy realized just in time that she was being teased and threw a pillow at her cousin. "Just because three inches looks better on me than on you!" she said.

"I didn't notice Peter complaining about the way I looked in a bikini," Caroline retorted. As soon as the words were out, she looked startled that she'd said them. "I'm sorry. That was dumb of me, Chrissy."

Chrissy shrugged and grinned broadly. "That's okay, Cara. I just went after Peter because he was the cutest counselor at the camp. And after the stupid way I acted, you deserved him. Besides, the moment Jeff came back into the picture, I forgot all about Peter."

"Yeah, and I guess he forgot about me," Caroline said. She sounded as if she didn't care too much, but Chrissy couldn't always tell how her cousin really felt inside.

"You still haven't heard from him?" she asked.

Caroline shook her head. "Not one word, but you know, I had a feeling that we wouldn't be writing to each other much. Peter was definitely one of those vacation romances that are destined to fizzle out once you get home. He was nice, but he wasn't . . . " She let her voice trail off.

"Luke," Chrissy supplied.

Caroline looked at her in surprise. "How did you know what I was thinking?"

"It's kind of obvious," Chrissy replied with a grin. "You do get a certain look on your face when you're thinking about Luke."

Caroline flushed. "I don't know why I'm still pining for him," she said. "After all, he's in Iowa and I'm here, so what's the use? We'll probably never see each other again."

"Poor Cara," Chrissy said softly. "We've both had a year of ups and downs, haven't we?"

"You can say that again," Caroline agreed with a sigh. "But I think I'm getting better at handling them. I can already look back on Peter as a fond memory." she paused. "Which reminds me— here!" She tossed a thick envelope into Chrissy's lap.

Chrissy took one look at it and squealed with delight. "The camp photos! You got them back! I can't wait to see them." She fumbled, trying to open the package too quickly. "Are they good? Did you get one of Elizabeth falling in the mud? Are there any of the costume party?"

"You'll see," Caroline said. "Luckily, they all

came out. I think they're pretty good, personally."

"Hey, you're right!" Chrissy said, grinning delightedly as she browsed through the photos. "Look at this one of Peter throwing you in the lake. You didn't take that one, I'll bet!"

Caroline laughed. "Brandon took it, remember? I gave him my camera to hold and he snapped the picture, the rat."

"It's pretty good. You can see how cute Peter looks when he's up to no good. What a great photo to pass around school! Oh, and here's Elizabeth!" Chrissy gave a great whoop of laughter. "Terrific! Look at all the mud. I loved that tug of war. That was my favorite moment of the whole camp. Hey, and here are your little angels in their costumes. Don't they look sweet? Did you get a shot after the whipped cream fight? Oh, you did!" Chrissy leaped up from the bench. "I've got an idea! Let's go right over and show these to Tracy. They'll give her a good laugh."

Caroline's face clouded over. "Chrissy," she said. "Do you think that's a good idea? I mean, the poor girl had to miss out on being at camp herself because of mono. How would you like to see pictures of your friends having fun when you were stuck in your own room all summer?"

"But Tracy's dying to see them," Chrissy insisted. "She asked me again when I talked to her on the phone last night. She wants to be a counselor next summer, you know, so she wants to see what the camp looks like for herself. . . ."

Caroline hesitated. "I think maybe we should

wait a while until she's completely on her feet again. She still looked pretty weak to me when we were over there last time."

"But these will give her spirits a lift," Chrissy said confidently. "Tracy keeps saying she can't wait to see what Peter and Elizabeth look like."

"Well, if you think we really should," Caroline said slowly. "I just hope they'll cheer her up and not make her more depressed."

"These photos would make anybody feel better," Chrissy said. "Look at this kid's face after the melon-eating contest!"

Caroline peered over her cousin's shoulder. "Now here's one that will definitely make Tracy laugh," she said, tapping Chrissy lightly on the shoulder. "Didn't I take a great shot of you with poison oak?"

"Don't you dare show her that one," Chrissy said, trying to pull the photo out of Caroline's grasp. "I look terrible, Cara, like a human radish."

"You were the one who said you wanted to make Tracy laugh," Caroline pointed out sweetly. She turned and headed up the last few steps toward the apartment house. "This one will do it, Chrissy!" she tossed back over her shoulder.

"Oh, all right. I'll let her see me looking like the curse of the beetroot mummy," Chrissy grumbled. "Let's go over to Tracy's right now, okay?" she called.

Caroline stopped halfway through the front door. "Christina Madden, I am not walking down the street with you dressed like that. You'd be arrested for sure, and three arrests in one year wouldn't look too good on your college applications!"

"You do exaggerate," Chrissy said, picking up her mother's letter and following Caroline into the house. "There was only one real arrest and that was for a good cause. I helped save the park by stealing a bulldozer. So what? Everyone thought I did a terrific thing, even the principal. The other time was a case of mistaken identity. I was only climbing back into my own room!"

Caroline giggled. "I know," she said. "But walking down the hill in that bikini would not be mistaken identity. It'd be indecent exposure."

"I think my exposure is very decent," Chrissy said, pushing past Caroline and up to their apartment, "but I was intending to go change, anyway, so hold your horses."

Chrissy reappeared almost instantly, clad in an oversized Mickey Mouse T-shirt—a souvenir of their trip to Disneyland. "Okay, let's go," she called, jumping past Caroline. "Last one down the steps is a rotten egg!"

"No fair!" Caroline protested. "You got a head start!"

"What is this intolerable noise?" Mrs. Langdon's voice echoed in the stairway from the second floor.

The girls looked at each other and grinned as they ran out into the sunlight.

"Do you realize that I never got into trouble

until *you* arrived?" Caroline hissed as they turned into the street.

"I know," Chrissy replied smugly. "You must have had such a boring life!"

"True," Caroline agreed. "It will sure seem quiet around here after you've gone home."

"I could always stay, if you're going to miss me so terribly," Chrissy teased.

"That's very sweet of you," Caroline countered with a grin. "But I'm also going to enjoy being able to get into the bathroom without a fight every morning."

"And I'm going to be competing with three horrible brothers for one bathroom," Chrissy said with a big sigh. "A nice, clean bathroom without boys' socks all over it is only one of the things I'm going to miss. It's going to be terrible not having you around. And I'll miss Tracy, too."

Caroline nodded. "Tracy's a great friend to have. Remember, Chrissy," she added, giving her cousin a warning look, "try not to babble on too much about all the fun things we did at camp. I know Tracy will be pretty down and she doesn't always tell anyone when she's upset. We'll just have to be very tactful."

"I'll try to remember not to be too overly excited," Chrissy agreed as they turned onto Tracy's block. "We'll have to keep stressing what a lot of good things she's got to look forward to next year. It's up to us to cheer her up, Cara."

Caroline glanced at her cousin again. "I'm not all that sure about your methods of cheering people up," she said. "A lot of things you do turn out to be hazardous. Remember the time you lassoed Peter and Elizabeth at camp?"

"You don't have to mention that little story to Tracy," Chrissy said quickly. "Or the time I pretended to drown and Elizabeth rescued me instead of Peter."

"I can see I've got some great opportunities for blackmail here," Caroline said with a grin, stepping forward to ring Tracy's doorbell. "Its a real shame you won't be around long enough for me to use them."

Tracy's little sister, Terri opened the door. "She's up in her room," she said, waving toward the stairs.

The girls looked worried. "Is she feeling worse again?" Caroline asked.

Terri shrugged. "I don't know," she said, wandering back down the hall.

"Poor Tracy," Caroline whispered as they crept up the stairs. "And remember, Chrissy—cool it. Don't be your usual loud, insufferable self, okay?"

Chrissy nodded and they tapped on the door.

"Terri, go away," came the voice on the other side. "You can't borrow my shoes."

"It's not Terri. It's Chrissy and Caroline," Chrissy called through the closed door. "May we come in?"

The door was opened. "Hi, guys!" Tracy shrieked, leaping out to give them both huge hugs. "I've been trying to call you two all morning. You must be psychic or something! Come on in. I can't wait to tell you. . . ." She jumped over a pile of clothes and landed on her bed with an almighty crash.

Chrissy glanced sideways at her cousin. "Quiet? Weak? Depressed?" she muttered. "Were we talking about the same Tracy Wong?"

Caroline giggled. "You look like you've made a miraculous recovery, Tracy," she said, perching herself on the end of the bed as Chrissy took the window seat. "Have they come up with a new drug for mono or something? When I left here yesterday you were lying in your bed, watching TV and moaning."

"I just got some great news," Tracy said, looking from Chrissy to Caroline. "My parents were worried that I wasn't getting better fast enough, so they phoned my aunt last night and asked her if I could go and stay with her until I got my strength back. My aunt said YES!"

"That's great, Tracy." Chrissy beamed. "You must be really close to your aunt."

"Are you kidding?" Tracy asked, wrinkling her nose. "My aunt is super-strict. I have to be in by ten o'clock when I stay with her. But . . ."

"But what?" Caroline pressed.

"She lives in Hawaii. Who would turn down a couple of weeks in Hawaii?"

"Wow!" Chrissy exclaimed. "You lucky thing. All those cute guys on the beach would make anyone take an interest in life again."

"If my aunt ever lets me go to the beach," Tracy said, rolling her eyes. "She probably won't let me out of her sight without a chaperone."

"Do you have cousins over there to hang around with?" Caroline asked.

Tracy shook her head. "My uncle and aunt don't have any kids. They're a nice quiet, elderly couple, unfortunately."

"Bummer drag," Chrissy said, trying out the phrase she'd picked up from some of her campers. "I guess Caroline and I had better come along to keep you company then, right, Cara?"

"Hey, wait a minute," Tracy exclaimed. "Why *don't* you guys come along? That would be fantastic!"

Caroline made a face. "And all our college money would go right down the drain."

"But it wouldn't cost that much," Tracy insisted, leaping up from the bed excitedly. "Just your fare and spending money. You could eat and sleep at my aunt's house."

"Right," Caroline said with a grin. "Your aunt will really want to put up with two strange girls, as well as her niece."

"I'm sure she wouldn't mind," Tracy said. "After all, if you two were there, she wouldn't have to worry about letting me out alone. I know she'd let me go to the beach with my nice, reliable friends to look after me."

Caroline snorted with laughter, but Chrissy had wriggled off the window seat. "I don't know what you're laughing about," she said to her cousin. "I think it's a *terrific* idea. We'd be great chaperones for Tracy, we'd be able to help her to meet all the cutest boys and . . . holy cow!"

"What?" The other girls demanded as Chrissy broke off with a wild yell.

"Do you know who's in Hawaii right now? I can't believe it—my dreams are all coming true! Jeff is actually there with his band! I'll be able to stroll down moonlit beaches, hand in hand with Jeff, just as I imagined it."

Tracy shook her head, smiling. "You haven't met my aunt yet. You and Jeff and my aunt will be strolling down the beaches together."

"I don't even care," Chrissy said, beginning to pace the room like a caged panther. "Just being with Jeff again would be the most wonderful thing in the world. You know, I was so depressed because I thought we wouldn't be able to spend much time together before I leave, and now suddenly, out of the blue, wham! All my wishes are answered. I must have a fairy godmother someplace. Let's call your aunt right now, Tracy, and ask her if Cara and I can come along, too. Come on, I'll help you dial."

"Chrissy!" Caroline touched her cousin lightly on the arm. "Hold on a minute, okay? Come down to earth."

"What's the matter?" Two worried faces turned to stare at Caroline.

"We need to do some thinking about this whole thing, that's all," Caroline said, sitting back on the bed and fiddling nervously with her hands. "We can't just go rushing off to Hawaii, you know.

Your folks are expecting you back home, Chrissy, and besides, you told me a few minutes ago that you were going to save every penny from now on for college."

"That was before we started talking about going to Hawaii," Chrissy said. "I'd rather slave for the rest of my life just to get the chance to go to Hawaii and be with Jeff."

"Oh, come on, Chrissy," Caroline said, laughing nervously. "Think this over logically. You *do* need money for college, and I thought you were going to hang around here until Jeff gets back."

"But that's nowhere near as good as being with him in Hawaii!" Chrissy replied, her eyes shining. "It's easy for *you* to say. You've been to Hawaii before, I haven't. This might be the only chance I'll ever have to go."

"Come on, Caroline," Tracy joined in. "What's the matter? Don't you want to come with me?"

"Of course I do, Tracy," Caroline said, "but I'm trying to think of the future, too. I need money for college as much as Chrissy does. I don't want my choice of schools to be limited by how close they are to home. The airfare to Hawaii alone would take a big bite out of my earnings."

"But you'll still be working at the music store this year, won't you?" Tracy asked. "You'll make back the money you spend in Hawaii."

"I guess so," Caroline said slowly. "Don't get me wrong. I'd love to go on vacation right now, but . . ."

"Fine," Chrissy said. "*I'll* go with Tracy and you

can stay home and save money. We'll be just fine without you. It'll be great in the surf, getting swept away by giant waves and eaten by giant sharks. They'll probably send you back the part of my bikini that they found washed up on the beach. You'll look at it and say, "If only I'd gone along to take care of Chrissy. If only . . ."

"Oh, all right," Caroline said, thumping her hands down on the soft comforter. "You've talked me into it. I'll go. But I think you guys are jumping the gun a little here. Tracy's aunt might say no flat out and then you'll really be disappointed. Besides, we have to ask our parents, too. We can't just take off."

"I'm sure my aunt will agree, Cara," Tracy assured her. "She's a very nice lady, even if she *is* old-fashioned. She'd like me to bring my two best friends, I know she would."

"And I'm sure my parents won't mind as long as I pay for it myself," Chrissy said. "I'm sure your parents probably feel the same way, Cara."

"I'll get Mom to call Aunt Hattie when she gets home. Hey, this is so exciting. We'll go surfing and snorkeling . . ."

"And go to beach parties and get the world's greatest suntan," Chrissy continued, going over to sit beside Caroline on the bed. "Come on, Cara. Aren't you just the teeny-weeniest bit excited?"

A big smile began to spread across Caroline's face. "Just a teeny bit," she agreed, jumping up. "Come on, Chrissy, let's go home and decide

what clothes we have that would be right to take
to Hawaii. We'll have to buy lots of new outfits,
I'm sure."

Chrissy and Tracy exchanged looks. "And who
was just going on about being careful with
money and saving every penny for college?"
Tracy asked. All the girls laughed.

"Anyway, Cara," Chrissy reminded her cousin,
"You've forgotten why we came here in the first
place. We got the camp pictures back. Tracy,
you've *got* to see Cara being thrown into the
lake."

"No you don't, Tracy," Caroline said, wrestling
with Chrissy for the photos. "You've got to see
Chrissy as the human radish."

Tracy laughed and grabbed the pictures away
from both of them. "I'll look at them all," she
said, "and I want to hear all about camp. I wasn't
really keen on hearing about it when you guys
first came home, to tell you the truth, but now
I'm feeling much better. So tell me—who's this
person lying face down in the mud?"

Caroline and Chrissy squealed with laughter.
"That's Elizabeth!" they both said at once.

"You know, the head counselor we wrote to
you about," Chrissy told her. "We had a tug of
war and, by secret agreement, everyone let go
except Elizabeth. She went flying into the mud,
and it was *wonderful*."

Tracy flipped wistfully through the photos.
"You two seem to have a great time wherever
you go."

"Which is why you need us around in Hawaii," Chrissy said warmly. "Hey, let me show you Peter. I tried to chase him, but for some strange reason, probably defective eyesight, he preferred Cara. This will give you some idea of the type of boys we can find for you on the beach."

"Wow," Tracy said, peering closely at the photograph. "Imagine a whole beachful of boys like that. I'm ready to pack my bags right now."

"Me, too," Chrissy said, grabbing Caroline's arm. "But maybe just a little shopping before we go . . ."

Tracy and Caroline started to laugh and, before long, Chrissy was laughing right along with them.

Chapter 3

"I can't get over the fact that we're actually on our way to Hawaii," Chrissy said, leaning across Caroline to peer out the window for the thousandth time. Once again she saw the blue ocean spread out beneath them, and she sank back into her seat with a contented sigh. "They'll never believe this back home," she said. "Plain old Chrissy Madden now a world-class jet setter. Even airplane travel is old hat to—" Chrissy stopped talking and clutched the arms of her seat as the plane took a sudden dip. "Holy cow, what was *that*?" she asked in a shaky voice.

"Only an air pocket," Caroline said calmly. "It's nothing."

"It sure felt like something to me," Chrissy

complained. "It felt like the roller coaster at Disneyland."

Tracy and Caroline both laughed. "Weren't you just saying that airplane travel is old hat," Tracy asked.

"Well, it's not that old," Chrissy replied sheepishly. "I'm going to hold on tightly to the arm rests in case another one comes up," she said.

"You should have been in Luke's plane when we got caught in that blizzard back in Iowa," Caroline began, a serious expression on her face. "That was *really* like being on a roller coaster."

"Wow, that must have been so scary," Tracy said.

"It was," Caroline agreed, turning back to the window with a faraway look in her eyes.

Chrissy and Tracy exchanged glances. It seemed as if Caroline was never going to get over Luke. Whenever anyone mentioned him, she went into a dream world of her own. Since Luke, Caroline had gone out with a few different guys, but none had been able to put Luke out of her head. Even Peter had been only a temporary distraction. Luke was as much on Caroline's mind as ever.

Who would ever have imagined it? Chrissy thought, staring at Caroline's neat, braided hair in wonder. *The first love of her life is a crop duster from Iowa whose family raises pigs! I should have been the one to fall for him. Instead, I'm crazy about a sophisticated musician from San Francisco who seemed to be just right for*

Caroline at first. Love is the weirdest thing!

The thought of Jeff sent Chrissy back into her own daydreams. Pretty soon the moment she'd dreamed of would arrive and she'd be seeing Jeff again. He'd be so surprised to see her! His eyes would focus on her across a crowded room and . . . Chrissy jerked abruptly back to the present. Would Jeff be pleased to see her? What if he wasn't? What if he had another girl in Hawaii and told her to get lost? Misery replaced the pink cloud she had been floating on. She wished she'd been able to notify him beforehand, but, of course, there had been no return address on the postcard. *I must be careful,* she warned herself. *No more rushing ahead without thinking the way I usually do or I might lose Jeff forever. I've got to plan it so that he's pleased to see me.*

She leaned across Caroline again to peer out the window.

"I'll tell you when I can see something, Chrissy," Caroline said. "We have another hour of traveling, so you won't see any islands for a while yet. They look very small from the air. You'll only catch a glimpse just before you land."

"I can't wait," Chrissy said with an excited sigh. "I've never seen a tropical island before. Will it be just like Gilligan's Island, do you think?"

Caroline and Tracy looked at each other and giggled.

"Honestly, Chrissy, you are one of a kind," Tracy remarked.

Chrissy sat up straight in her seat and grinned.

"Well, thank you, Tracy. I take that as a compliment." She picked up the in-flight magazine from the pocket on the back of the seat in front of her and pretended to concentrate.

At last Caroline touched her arm excitedly. "Look!" she whispered. "Down there."

Chrissy leaned across to look out the window. The plane had dipped a wing to make a gentle turn and suddenly there was the island of Oahu beneath them. "Oh, wow!" Chrissy blurted out. "It's just like all the postcards! That's Waikiki, isn't it? There, look—you can see the beach and the hotels and the palm trees. . . and is that Diamond Head? Holy cow, look at the crater—is it still active? I don't want to be swept away by lava one night. . . ."

"Chrissy!" Caroline interrupted. "Half the plane doesn't want to hear your commentary, and you're squashing me."

"Sorry, Cara," Chrissy said, moving back half an inch. "It's just that you know I get carried away when I'm excited and this is like a dream come true."

Down below the ocean went from deepest peacock blue to pale turquoise as the plane neared the shore. Toward the beach the smooth surface seemed to be pleated with waves. Chrissy grabbed Caroline's arm. "Look—you can actually see the waves coming into shore. What are those little black dots, Cara? Hey, I know what they are—they must be surfers! There are real-live surfers below us, Cara, and one of them might even be Jeff! Jeff! Hi!!! I'm coming, Jeff."

"Chrissy!" Caroline whispered into her ear.

"Okay. Sorry. I'll shut up. I'll try not to be excited," Chrissy said sheepishly, "even though this is the most exciting moment of my life. I'll just sit here quietly and say nothing."

She leaned back in her seat and folded her arms. Caroline laughed. "You are an idiot," she said. "Of course, you can still look, but try not to yell so much. I don't want everyone to think we are first-time tourists."

"I can't help being a first-time tourist," Chrissy said, "and I'm so excited I think I'll explode."

She riveted her eyes on the beach and the surfers. In a few moments she'd be down there among them, down on that beach getting a great tan and having fun. What a perfect end to an amazing year! To think that last summer she'd spent her days swimming in the creek and having picnics with Ben, which she'd thought was the ultimate summer. Coming to California sure had changed her life, and this trip to Hawaii was the crowning moment—one that would make her the envy of all the kids in Danbury when she got home. "My great tan? Oh, I got that in Hawaii. Would you like to see a picture of me surfing?" she would say.

The ocean rose up to meet the plane. They were skimming along, inches over the sparkling blue-green surface. Then there was a runway beneath them and the wheels touched down on the island of Oahu.

"I hope Aunt Hattie still recognizes me," Tracy said as they walked across the blacktop from the plane to the airport terminal. "I haven't seen her in three years and I know I've changed a lot. When I was here last I was chubby and had braces."

"You'll recognize her," Caroline reminded her friend. She led Tracy and Chrissy into the terminal. "She won't have changed in three years."

"You're right," Tracy said. "There she is now!" She broke into a run. "Aunt Hattie! It's Tracy!"

Chrissy and Caroline watched her run over to a tiny Chinese woman, no more than five feet tall, and engulf her in a hug. This is Tracy's super-strict aunt? Chrissy mused. She didn't look anything like the big mean ogre Chrissy had imagined. This woman looked frail enough to be blown away by the wind.

Tracy turned back toward the cousins and beckoned them to join her. "Aunt Hattie, Uncle Albert," she said grandly. "I want you to meet my best friends. This is Caroline and this is Chrissy."

Aunt Hattie smiled shyly and nodded her head. Uncle Albert, a tall, studious-looking man with glasses, extended a hand to Chrissy. "Aloha," he said.

"Hello-ha," Chrissy mumbled back.

"That means welcome," Tracy interrupted. "It also means good-bye."

Chrissy felt that she was grinning like an idiot. She hadn't expected a language barrier in Hawaii.

Tracy's uncle leaned toward his niece and whispered something. Tracy nodded. "That's a nice idea," she said. She turned to her friends. "Uncle Albert wants to get you a lei."

"Oh, that's lovely," Caroline said instantly.

"Oh, yes, lovely," Chrissy echoed, though she had no idea what they were talking about. She sure had a lot to learn about Hawaii, she decided, following the others until they stopped by a flower stand. Uncle Albert pointed to three flower garlands. The woman handed them to him after he paid her and he came toward Chrissy first.

"Aloha, Chrissy," he said, stepping toward her. Chrissy stepped back and held out her hands for the flowers. The others laughed.

"He wants to put the lei around your neck, Chrissy," Tracy told her. "That's the traditional Hawaiian way."

"Oh," Chrissy said, feeling her cheeks turn flaming pink. She smelled the sweet scent of the white flowers as Uncle Albert slipped them over her head. Then he did the same to Caroline and Tracy. Chrissy felt rather stupid, walking through a crowded airport with flowers around her neck, but she soon saw that many other travelers had them, too, and that people waiting to welcome visitors often carried leis ready to greet the new arrivals. Even as they walked through the airport, Chrissy was conscious that she was somewhere new and exciting. The airport terminal was open at the sides and gardens grew between the gates. The air was hot and heady with strange scents that Chrissy could not identify, as if the whole island was blooming with exotic flowers.

Outside the terminal, they all squeezed into Tracy's uncle's sporty imported car and zoomed off onto a modern, multi-laned freeway toward the high-rises of a city. While Tracy was carrying on a rapid conversation with her aunt, Chrissy concentrated on staying silent in the back seat. Usually when she was nervous or excited her tongue just ran away with her. Now she was determined not to embarrass Tracy in front of her aunt and uncle and she was sure to say something dumb if she opened her mouth.

Everything was so different from what she had imagined. Why, Honolulu didn't look very exotic—it just looked like a plain old city. Maybe Hawaii was just a big hoax! Maybe the beaches weren't even very nice when you saw them up close. Maybe the palm trees were just plastic . . . maybe Jeff wouldn't even . . . *now you are being just plain dumb,* she told herself. *You are tired after a long flight. No more negative thoughts. You are going to have the greatest time here and come back with a tan that everyone in Danbury will envy.*

The car drew up outside a pleasant-looking white apartment block with a colorful flower garden in front.

Why, there's nothing exotic about this place at all, Chrissy thought. *This building could be next door to us in San Francisco.* She opened the door and climbed out of the car, but as she stepped onto the sidewalk, she heard a deep, rumbling voice that sounded like it came from a loudspeaker.

"Aloha. Welcome to the sunny shores of Hawaii. I am sure you will have a fantastic time here."

Chrissy looked up to find herself face to stomach with a man in a white uniform. She craned her neck back as far as it would go until she found a pair of friendly brown eyes gazing down at her in amusement.

The man extended his hand to Chrissy, but she was so overwhelmed that she simply stood there, staring up at him in awe.

"Chrissy, that's Wilfred, the doorman," Tracy said, squeezing out of the car behind her.

"Aloha, Miss Tracy," Wilfred said, beaming at Tracy as if she were his long-lost daughter.

"Hi, Wilfred, you remember me?" she asked.

"Sure I remember you, only last time you were here you were always eating," he said with his rumbling laugh. "I think you found out about boys and diets since you were here last because you've grown up real pretty!"

Caroline was last to climb from the car and stood on the sidewalk beside Chrissy. "Mama mia, I've never seen anyone so huge!" she whispered to Chrissy as Wilfred unloaded their cases from the trunk. "He must be over seven feet tall!"

Chrissy smiled at her cousin and nodded. She felt instantly much better knowing that Caroline was right beside her.

Chapter 4

"Come on," Chrissy whispered to Caroline. "Let's go inside. What we both need is a cool drink." She helped Caroline carry her case through the glass front door into a marble entrance hall. Tracy's aunt and uncle had the first-floor apartment, with a small garden out back full of scented, blooming trees. A tree covered with white flowers was blossoming outside their bedroom window. A fan turned lazily on their ceiling and the tiled floors felt cool beneath the thin soles of their sandals. Chrissy suddenly found herself yawning, her whole body drained of energy.

"Are you young ladies going to take a nap while I fix dinner?" Aunt Hattie demanded.

"If you're sure you don't want any help in the kitchen?" Chrissy asked.

Aunt Hattie eyed her critically as if she already suspected that Chrissy's talents in the kitchen were limited. "I like to keep my kitchen to myself," she said firmly. "My husband will tell you that I throw things at him if he so much as puts his face through the door."

Uncle Albert laughed good-naturedly. "So you girls don't bother getting up if you hear pots and pans crashing around, okay?"

A nap in that cool, sweet-smelling bedroom did seem like an inviting thought, until Tracy interrupted her aunt and uncle. "Come on, Aunt Hattie, they can't possibly take a nap until they've seen the ocean," Tracy said. Chrissy's sagging energy returned instantly at the thought of seeing the famous beach.

"Is it far to the beach?" Caroline asked.

"Only three blocks," Aunt Hattie replied. "You go for a walk before dinner then and get up an appetite. What do you like to eat?"

"How about a nice bowl of poi?" Uncle Albert suggested.

"Oh, sure, poi will do nicely," Chrissy said politely.

Tracy grinned at her aunt and uncle. "Somehow I don't think she'll like it much."

"You know what poi tastes like, young lady?" Uncle Albert asked Chrissy. "It tastes like wallpaper paste! I think we'll stick to normal food, Hattie, and forget the poi."

The girls left the apartment and walked past Wilfred who raised a giant hand in greeting. Outside they dissolved into noisy laughter.

"You are funny, Chrissy," Tracy said. "You didn't really think they were going to offer you poi, did you?"

"Well, er . . . of course not," Chrissy lied. "Which direction is the beach?" she asked rapidly, changing the subject.

The three blocks seemed to stretch on forever in the oppressive evening heat. Then they turned a final corner and found themselves on a busy main street. The street was lined with tall buildings, and the sidewalks were jammed with pedestrians, all wearing Hawaiian print shirts, mumus, and dresses. Stores on either side of them were bursting with exciting things to buy—gold-dipped leaves, unusual jewelry, and bright swimwear. Island music was playing in many of them and it blended well with the ringing of bicycle bells as pedicabs rode past them, mostly pedaled by cute, tanned boys. Between the buildings were alleyways crammed with stalls full of gold chains and charms, carved coral, Chinese enamel, and leather purses.

"Come on, young ladies, every oyster has a pearl in it," a vendor called, pointing to a tank beside him.

The girls looked at each other and grinned excitedly.

"It's like stepping into a gold mine, isn't it?"

Tracy asked. "What a good thing we didn't bring our money with us, or we'd have spent all of it in ten minutes."

"Did you see how cheap that gold chain was?" Caroline asked.

"And those pretty gold leaves?" Chrissy joined in. "Only a dollar each—I've got to take some back as souvenirs."

"Come on, you guys. We can browse another time," Tracy said, slipping between them and pushing them gently away from a stall. "I want to see the sun set over the ocean."

The girls allowed themselves to be swept forward by Tracy, until they passed the last hotel and there before them was the ocean. The wide sandy beach was almost empty at this time in the evening, with just a few determined surfers lying like seals on boards beyond the break of waves and a few couples strolling hand in hand along the water's edge. Chrissy gave a big sigh of contentment. "It's perfect," she said.

The fiery red sun was already sinking rapidly behind the wispy clouds on the horizon. As the girls watched from beneath a row of palm trees, the sun illuminated each cloud in turn until it reached the rim of the sea and dropped into the water behind it.

"That was the most fantastic sunset I've ever seen," Chrissy remarked to the other two, "and you get some pretty dramatic sunsets back in Iowa after a storm. Was it my imagination or does the sun fall faster here?"

Caroline smiled. "It certainly seemed that way, didn't it? You could actually watch it fall into the ocean."

"That's impossible. The sun sets at the same speed no matter where you are," Tracy said seriously. "Because the earth rotates at the same speed everywhere."

Chrissy glanced at Caroline and saw that she was grinning, too. "Tracy, be quiet!" they said in unison and burst out laughing.

"From now on there will be no more scientific principles, Tracy Wong," Chrissy said firmly. "We are on the island of romance and if strange and wonderful things happen, I don't want them explained away for me."

Tracy laughed, too. "I have to admit, it is pretty romantic here," she said. "Look at that girl down at the water's edge in that white lace skirt. Doesn't she look like something out of a dream sequence in a movie?"

"More like a deodorant commercial," Chrissy said.

"Now who's being unromantic?" Tracy quipped back.

Chrissy started giggling. "I guess it will seem more romantic when that girl is me and I'm strolling along that beach with Jeff," she said.

"So are you going to call him tonight?" Tracy asked.

Chrissy felt her cheeks flush. "No. I don't know exactly where he is—all I know is that his band is playing at some place in Waikiki, that begins with a B. I couldn't make out what he wrote on his postcard."

"Why don't you look it up in the phone book?" Caroline suggested. "I'm sure you could figure it out that way. Should be a piece of cake."

"Speaking of cake," Chrissy interrupted, ignoring her cousin's suggestion. She did want to see Jeff, but she had to admit to herself that she was afraid. "I hate to say it, but I'm starving."

"You were the only one who ate your meal on the flight," Caroline said in mock horror. "Your stomach is like a bottomless pit."

"I can't help it that I was born with a healthy appetite," Chrissy said. "Do you know what your aunt has planned for dinner, Tracy?"

"Oh, I expect she'll do her specialty for the first night here," Tracy said seriously. "Hundred-year-old eggs and bird's nest soup." She caught Chrissy's worried glance at Caroline and burst out laughing. "I'm kidding, you dope," she said. "I'm sure we'll eat perfectly normal food, although I had hundred-year-old eggs once and they weren't half bad—pretty salty but you don't even taste the egg."

"The egg was really a hundred years old?" Caroline asked in disgust.

"More like three months, I think," Tracy said. "The hundred-year bit is just their name. They bury them in the ground and they come out all black."

"*Euuwww!*" Caroline and Chrissy said at the same time.

They started to walk back along the main street, getting jostled by the crowds of people who were entering hotels and restaurants for their evening meal. Music was spilling from open doorways and the atmosphere was of a giant festival. Suddenly Chrissy grabbed Caroline's arm. "Listen," she said.

"To what?" Caroline paused and looked around.

"That music coming from that courtyard. That has got to be Jeff's band. Doesn't that sound like their lead guitar?"

Caroline listened and nodded. Chrissy gave a whoop of delight. "Look at the sign! Appearing in the Banyan Court, The Earthquakes! Oh, jeepers!"

"You want to go take a look?" Tracy asked. "The Banyan Court's really something. I came with my family once. Come on, I'll show you."

She walked through a big archway with palm trees on either side of it, followed by Chrissy and Caroline.

"Isn't this a hotel?" Caroline whispered. "Are we allowed in here?"

"Sure we are. The Banyon Court is a regular lounge, but it's really different . . . look—see what I mean?"

They had crossed a tiled foyer and now found themselves standing in a large open area in the middle of the hotel. The area was dotted with little tables arranged in a circle where customers sat sipping huge, exotic-looking drinks from coconut shells, while the waitresses rustled about in their grass skirts. In the center of the circle was a huge banyan tree. A little hut had been built about ten feet up in the branches of the tree and a rope bridge linked the hut to a series of ladders. Giant arial roots fell from the branches to bury themselves in the floor below, making the bottom branches look like old men's knobbled arms supported by thick canes. All the branches were strung with rows of miniature lights that winked on and off, creating an impression of a magic tree from a story.

"Wow," Caroline said, obviously impressed.

Chrissy said nothing. She was very conscious of the music coming from the stage behind the tree. Any moment now the song would end, then she would walk around that giant trunk and Jeff would look up ... their eyes would meet and ... Suddenly Chrissy began to feel panic rising up inside her. What if a big smile of delight and surprise didn't spread across his face? What if he felt trapped by a girl who followed him halfway across the world? What if he'd already found another girl over here? She grabbed Tracy's arm. "Let's get out of here," she whispered. "I don't want him to see me right now."

She turned and pushed past a group of people arriving at the doorway. She ran across the tiled foyer and out past the palm trees. Then she hurried down the block, dodging among the sunburnt tourists in her haste to get away. The other two girls hurried to catch up with her.

"Chrissy, what on earth's the matter with you?" Caroline asked. "I thought you came to Hawaii so you could see Jeff?"

"I did," Chrissy said, panting as she hurried forward in the clammy evening heat.

"And you've just decided you don't want to anymore?" Caroline demanded.

"Of course not," Chrissy said, but she didn't slow down.

"So why are we running away like this?"

"Because," Chrissy replied, hurrying faster.

Caroline reached out and grabbed her cousin's arm to stop her. "Because is not a good enough reason," she snapped, glaring into Chrissy's innocent blue eyes. "Now, Chrissy Madden, you tell me what is wrong."

Chrissy wriggled her arm out of Caroline's grasp. "Cara, I want to be prepared to see him— I don't want him to see me just out of the blue like this."

"Why on earth not, Chrissy?"

"In case he's mad that I came here and he thinks I'm spying on him and chasing him and he doesn't want to see me again." Chrissy started walking again, but slower this time, with Caroline and Tracy on either side.

"Why should he be mad at you?" Caroline

asked. "I was in Reno with you, remember? He was certainly pleased to see you then."

"I know," Chrissy said, "but he was expecting to see me then. He even invited me. But he has no idea I came to Hawaii. I don't want to blow everything with him by appearing at the wrong moment. I want to make sure he's delighted to see me!"

"You sure are weird, Chrissy," Tracy said, shaking her head. "If the boy I was crazy about was just a few feet away like that, nothing in the world would stop me from going in to see him."

"Maybe if I were more sure of Jeff, it would be different," Chrissy said slowly. "I've never dated someone like him before. I only know good old Ben back home who was always there for me, always steady and reliable. But Jeff is unpredictable, and I guess that's partly why I'm attracted to him. But I'm also scared that Jeff might not want to be tied to one girl." She paused as they stopped at the red light, glancing over her shoulder as if she expected to see Jeff running behind her. "This needs some thinking out first," she said. "We've got to plan how and when Jeff and I should meet so that it seems like the most natural thing in the world. I'm going to need both of your brains to help me."

"And I thought I came to Hawaii for a rest, didn't you, Cara?" Tracy asked with a grin.

"We should have known," Caroline answered.

"Nothing is ever easy when Chrissy is around."

They both started giggling as they crossed the street, but Chrissy glanced over her shoulder one more time.

Chapter 5

Chrissy woke up very early the next morning. Lying on her cot in the dawn coolness, she was thinking much more clearly. Unfortunately, her conclusion was the same. She knew the others thought she was out of her mind to have panicked about meeting Jeff again, but even now she knew she had been right. *Timing is the key*, she decided. Some guys would be pleased to have a girl follow them to Hawaii, but she was sure that Jeff was not one of them. He was independent and free-spirited, and he'd said those were qualities he liked in Chrissy, too. *Sounds like a bald eagle*, she thought wryly, *but I guess I'm really just a great big chicken.*

In her head she kept imagining that she was waiting for Jeff at the back of the lounge. As he

played his drums, his eyes searched the room.
She waited for his eyes to meet hers, for the look
of amazement, then the big, wonderful smile. But
instead, his eyes stopped short and he winked at
a sultry Hawaiian girl who was leaning against a
pillar with a red flower in her hair. . . .

I've got to know where I stand, she decided, *or
rather where he stands. Maybe if I got Caroline
and Tracy to do a little detective work for me first
. . . That way I can plan an "accidental" meeting
that will be perfect. . . .*

She closed her eyes and ran the scene through
her head. She was lying on the beach, surrounded by surfing hunks, her tiny bikini con-
trasting with her perfect tan and her lovely sun-
bleached hair. Just as Jeff was walking by, she
would open her eyes and appear to notice him.
She would sit up in amazement.

"Jeff?"

"Chrissy? Is that really you? What on earth are
you doing here?"

"Just a little vacation with my friends. What are
you . . . oh, I remember now. You did tell me you
were playing in Hawaii. . . ."

Jeff would be on his knees beside her. "Chrissy,
this is the most amazing coincidence."

"Yes, isn't it?"

"I can't get over it."

"Me, neither. It's nice to see you, Jeff."

Jeff would reach out his hand and take hers.
"Come on, let's go for a walk. It's kind of crowded
around here. Who are all these guys, anyway?"

"Nobody special. Just guys I met on the beach."
Chrissy would get up and bid farewell to her
entourage of hunks. "I'll see you guys later. Much
later . . ."

The scene dissolved into another scene on the
beach, this time at sunset. She and Jeff are
walking hand in hand along beach. Jeff pauses to
kiss her as the sun plops into the ocean.

"Chrissy, this is the most amazing, wonderful
thing that ever happened to me," Jeff would say.
"We are going to have the greatest two weeks
together. . . ."

With this scene in mind, Chrissy got out of bed,
showered, and began to pack her beach bag.
Caroline moaned and turned over.

"Chrissy, what are you doing? It's the middle of
the night," she groaned.

"No, it isn't. It's eight o'clock and I'm all set to
go down to the beach. I've just decided I've got to
get the world's greatest tan in a hurry so that I
look better than all the Hawaiian beauties."

Caroline opened her eyes and focused on
Chrissy. "You are funny sometimes. Do you want
this great tan to impress Jeff?"

"Of course. There is a lot of competition on this
island. I want to make sure I am looking my
adorable, sexy best when we meet."

Caroline sat up and yawned. "And have you
decided where and when you are finally going to
meet him? Have you gotten up the courage to go
down to the Banyan Court tonight?"

"I was sort of hoping," Chrissy said, looking

down at her bare toes sticking out of her thongs, "that you and Tracy might do a little snooping for me first."

"Oh, yes?" Caroline asked, raising an eyebrow, "You want us to crawl in through his dressing-room window? Follow him home? Interrogate his friends?"

"Nothing like that," Chrissy protested. She knew her cousin was teasing, but this was important. "I just thought that you might meet him first and sort of mention that I was here, too . . . just to check out his reaction. You could also keep an eye out for another girl hanging around."

"And if he does have another girl, what then?" Caroline asked.

Chrissy wrinkled her nose. "I guess I'd try to understand and realize that some things are not meant to last."

"You would?" Caroline asked in amazement.

Chrissy grinned. "No way," she said. "I'd throw her into one of the Hawaiian volcanos!"

"That's what I thought," Caroline said, smiling, too. "I remember the poor girl you pushed into that heap of pies because she was chasing Ben. Heaven help any girl who is after Jeff!"

"All the same," Chrissy said, "it was different with Ben. He'd been my steady guy for years and years. I had a right to push Tammy into the pies. Jeff isn't the steady type and I know it. I have to be very careful that I don't come across as the little lovesick farm girl who's going to chase him clear across the world. I don't want to scare the guy off."

"So you're going to get a tan to make sure he likes you best?" Caroline asked in a doubtful voice. "You think that will do it?"

"The tan is just part of it," Chrissy said, cramming more items into her beach bag as she talked. "My itsy-bitsy bikini and a whole gang of gorgeous guys around me might help, too. It certainly wouldn't hurt to make Jeff feel jealous—make him realize what he's losing when I go back to Danbury."

"I must say, I've always admired your confidence," Caroline said.

"More like desperation," Chrissy replied. "I'm crazy about this guy, Cara, and this might be my last chance to be with him in my whole life. I want it to be a good chapter for my autobiography."

"Your autobiography?!" Caroline burst into laughter as Chrissy tried to look haughty and not amused.

"What's so funny?" Tracy mumbled, still half asleep in the next bed.

"Chrissy is going to write her autobiography," Caroline said.

"Oh, that's nice," Tracy said sleepily, as she pulled the covers over her head and went back to sleep.

"I'll see you down at the beach, Cara," Chrissy said. "I don't want to waste any precious sunshine."

"Don't overdo it," Caroline cautioned. "The sun is very strong here."

"I know," Chrissy said. "Don't worry. I've already got a good layer of tan from your front yard, and I've got loads of sunscreen and a big hat and a cover-up and a book to read and a pillow and a towel and . . . this bag is so darned heavy, I can hardly lift it!"

Chrissy surveyed the beach with discriminating eyes. This was the first phase in her set-up for Jeff, and she wanted to get off to a good start. *Ah hah!* She thought, *that looks like a good spot*, and she set her beach bag down right in the path of a surfer heading for the ocean. He was so intent on checking out the waves that he didn't notice Chrissy until he tripped over her bag.

"Oh, sorry," the boy apologized, picking himself up and brushing off the sand. Then he smiled at Chrissy and said, "Hi, haven't seen you here before. I'm Tod."

By the time Caroline and Tracy joined her, Chrissy had met all of Tod's friends, and was surrounded by boys.

Chrissy looked up and waved. "Over here, girls. This is a terrific beach. You meet so many friendly people. I know we're going to have a great time here."

Caroline and Tracy approached cautiously, as half a dozen suntanned boys turned to stare at them.

"These kids are all from California, too,"

Chrissy said happily. "Guys, this is my cousin Caroline and my friend Tracy. Cara and Tracy meet Tod and Brett and Chris and John and . . . I'm sorry, I keep forgetting your name."

The last guy gave an embarrassed smile, as if it was somehow his fault that Chrissy didn't remember him. "It's Jeremy," he mumbled.

Chrissy beamed and turned to Cara and Tracy. "This is Jeremy, girls. He's from Santa Barbara and you should see him surf."

Caroline and Tracy spread out their towels next to Chrissy and made polite conversation with the boys until they headed back into the ocean with their surfboards. The moment they were gone Caroline bombarded Chrissy.

"I must say, you don't waste any time, do you? How on earth did you manage it?"

Chrissy turned her large blue eyes on her cousin. "Me?" she asked innocently. "I didn't do a thing. I just sat here, minding my own business, and the boys just sort of appeared."

"I'll say they appeared," Tracy added. "You seem to have attracted all the hunks on the entire beach."

Chrissy grinned happily. "They are kind of cute, aren't they? Especially Tod, don't you think?"

"I thought the last one, Jeremy, was the cutest," Tracy said thoughtfully. "He seemed to a little shy. I like that."

"Funny. I thought that the one sitting behind me—was that Brett?—was definitely the best-looking. Those shoulders—wow! And that dark, mysterious look . . ."

Chrissy giggled. "It's a good thing everyone's definition of cute is different or we'd all be fighting over the same boy," she said. "But I do notice that once again Caroline goes for the one who looks most like Luke."

"Does he?" Caroline asked, surprised. "I didn't say I go for him. I was just commenting that he was the most interesting-looking—purely an objective opinion."

Tracy and Chrissy exchanged a glance. "My opinion was purely objective, too. Wasn't yours, Chrissy?" Tracy asked with a big smile.

"In my case it really was," Chrissy said. "All the while they were talking I was busy analyzing which of them was most likely to make Jeff jealous."

"Oh, come on, Chrissy," Caroline said firmly. "You can't think like that, and you can't go around manipulating people. No good ever comes of trying to force people into things. Think about summer camp and all the schemes you had to catch Peter. It didn't work, did it? It never works, Chrissy. You should have learned that by now."

"It's all very well for you to lecture," Chrissy said, "but I'd like to see what you'd do if Luke were here, interested in another girl, and you wanted to get him back."

"I don't know what I'd do," Caroline admitted hesitantly, her face clouding, "but since Luke isn't here and I probably won't ever see him again, let's not talk about him. Jeff is here and I think you should be open and honest with him. If you are dying to see him again, just wait around for him in the Banyan Court and say hello when you see him."

Chrissy made a face. "I'm scared, Cara," she said. "I'm so scared that he won't be happy to see me. What I'd like most in the world is to have two wonderful weeks with him. But I'm trying to be realistic." She picked up a handful of sand and watched as the white grains cascaded through her fingers. "Jeff and I were not exactly going steady. He likes me, I know, but I don't think he's as crazy about me as I am about him. I just want to think ahead about ways to get him back if he does have another girl over here, that's all . . . and making him jealous may do it."

"Not if you intend to use someone else to do it, Chrissy. That's not right," Tracy added.

"I'm not going to *use* anyone. I'm just being friendly, the way I always am. I'm not giving anybody the come-on."

"Just make sure it stays that way," Caroline said. "I know what happens to guys when you turn your big baby blue eyes on them."

"It didn't work with Peter," Chrissy said, giving Caroline a sly grin. "Your baby blue eyes worked much better."

"Hey, cut it out, you guys," Tracy interrupted. "You came here to be on vacation. In fact, you're supposed to be helping me recuperate, but all you're doing is bickering like little kids."

"Sorry," Caroline said. "Anyone coming for a swim?"

"Good idea," Tracy agreed. "Come on, lazybones." She kicked sand at Chrissy.

"I just need to finish my tanning first," Chrissy said. "I'm not a nice golden brown yet."

"Chrissy, you've been here for hours," Tracy warned. "Be careful you don't burn."

"I'm fine," Chrissy said. "We farm girls have tough skin. I'll know when I've had enough. I'll swim later. Tod has offered to give me surfing lessons when the waves quiet down this afternoon."

She lay back onto her towel while the others headed toward the ocean. Her best bet, she decided, was to have Cara talk to Jeff first. If he didn't seem absolutely thrilled to have her in Hawaii, then maybe the great tan and a whole bunch of cute guys around her would stimulate his interest. . . . Her thoughts became fuzzy as she drifted into sleep.

"Chrissy?"

She returned to consciousness as she heard her name. She opened her eyes. "Oh, hi, Cara. I guess I slept."

"You really should quit lying in the sun," Caroline said. "Go have a swim. Tracy and I just had a great time."

"We did not," Tracy said. "She saw a big wave coming and didn't warn me. I got dumped." She looked across at Caroline and laughed. "If my mother or my aunt could see our definition of taking it easy and recovering, they'd have a blue fit." She opened the umbrella and lay under it.

Chrissy got up. "I think I will have that swim," she said. Her shoulders and back were definitely feeling hot, but a glance over her shoulder did not show any redness and she gave a sigh of relief. *Chrissy Madden acquires world's greatest tan*, she thought. She pictured herself walking down the street in front of the Banyan Court wearing her white halter, getting admiring glances from all the newly arrived pale-faced mainlanders. Then Jeff would catch sight of her as he arrived for work. . . .

She took off her sunglasses and headed for the ocean, just as the boys were coming out, clutching their boards and laughing noisily. Tod stopped when he saw her. "Oh, Chrissy, want your lesson now?" he asked.

Chrissy eyed the waves nervously. She loved the beach, but she was still wary about swimming in the ocean. Never in all her life would she forget her first time in the ocean—with Caroline and all her friends—when a wave had knocked her over, and she'd thought for sure she was a goner. Even from the edge of the ocean the waves seemed to rush in fiercely.

"I've never tried this before," she began hesitantly. "Do you think—"

"The waves are real tame right now," Tod cut in. "You'll be fine."

Chrissy swallowed hard and gave a brave smile.

Knowing how to surf would be another scoring point when she met Jeff. "Okay, I guess," she said.

Tod grinned. "Great," he said. "Here, take my board, and I'll borrow Jeremy's. Let's go out past the breakers and then I'll show you how to get up on the board."

They started to wade out, pushing the boards ahead of them. The waves seemed even bigger as they slapped against the boards, throwing spray into Chrissy's face and taking her breath away. Tod didn't even seem to notice the waves as he strode effortlessly into deeper and deeper water. When Chrissy glanced back at the shore, it seemed very far away. Caroline and Tracy were only two pale dots under a miniature umbrella. Chrissy looked across at Tod and managed a smile.

"Now," Tod said, holding the board steady. "I want you to climb up and get the feel of it."

"On top of it, you mean?" Chrissy asked.

Tod laughed. "You can't surf underneath it. Just pull yourself on until you are lying on it, then kneel, and when you feel confident, stand."

He gave her an encouraging smile. *He's very cute*, Chrissy thought and gave him her best smile back. "Here goes," she said.

Chrissy dragged herself onto the slippery board, until she was lying on her stomach, then she carefully got to her knees.

"Now stand!" Tod commanded.

"There's nothing to hang on to!" Chrissy

shouted, as a wave flipped her into the water.

Tod laughed. "Not bad," he said. "You have to feel the water to keep your balance."

"We'll try it on a wave," Tod said. "The board won't wobble when it's moving forward. I want you to lie on the board like I showed you, then start paddling like crazy when I tell you to and I'll get you started. Okay?"

Chrissy wanted to say "Not okay" but she managed to nod again. After all, not every girl got surfing lessons from one of the cutest guys on the beach on her first day in Hawaii. She didn't want Tod and his buddies to think she was a wimp. Besides, she was proud of her record of trying anything once. She wanted to go back home and show them photos of her surfing, something that nobody in Danbury could do. She hoisted herself onto the board. "Okay," she said.

"Great," Tod said. He reached across his board to give her a friendly pat. "Now be ready. You have to get up speed at the right moment. Here comes a good one—ready, start paddling ... now!"

Tod gave an enormous push. Suddenly Chrissy felt the wave pick her up. She was rushing forward.

"Kneel up," Tod was yelling, "then gradually stand."

Very gently Chrissy got to her knees. Then she steadied herself on the surfboard and slowly stood up. People flashed past her. The shore rushed to meet her. She was actually riding a wave! A feeling of triumph shot through her. Chrissy Madden had managed to ride a wave the first time she surfed! Not bad for someone who could hardly swim when she arrived in California! She could see Caroline and Tracy, both standing now, watching her. She could see the other guys standing in the shallows, also watching and applauding. The shore came closer. Suddenly she realized that the wave she was riding was going to crash onto the shore very soon.

"How do you stop this thing?" she yelled.

"Just jump down and hold on to your board!" Jeremy called out, rushing toward her.

"I don't think I can!" she shouted.

"Then fall off and I'll grab the board!" Jeremy shouted back.

Fall off? But that's even scarier than staying on! she thought in a panic. Then she saw Brett swimming up to her with a big grin on his face.

"Here," he called, holding up a hand to her. She grabbed the hand and slithered off the board into his arms. She fought to regain her balance, flinging her arms around his neck as the wave threatened to sweep her on with it. As she stood up, Brett tightened his arms around her waist.

"This wasn't what I had in mind, but it's not half bad," he said, holding her tightly and grinning at her.

Chrissy gave an embarrassed smile and glanced back at the shore. As she turned her head, she froze. Someone was standing a few feet away, watching her intently. As her eyes met his, she saw recognition spread across his face.

"It *is* you, Chrissy," Jeff said. "I thought I was seeing a mirage when you came in on that board."

"Hi, Jeff," she began, conscious that Brett was still holding her. "I was just taking my first surfing lesson. . . ."

Just at that moment Tod came riding effortlessly in on the next wave.

"Hey, Brett!" he yelled. "Get your hands off her. She's mine!"

Jeff's eyes narrowed. He glanced up at Tod, at Brett, and then back to Chrissy. "Well, good seeing you, Chrissy," he said sharply. "I don't want to keep you from your surfing lesson!"

Then he turned and walked back up the beach, disappearing into the crowd before Chrissy could break free from Brett's embrace.

Chapter 6

"I feel so totally, utterly, completely miserable," Chrissy said with a sigh, turning her head toward Caroline as she lay stretched out on her stomach on her narrow cot. When they first arrived in Hawaii she had volunteered to take the cot so her cousin and friend could have the twin beds, but now she wished she had not been so generous. The cot was hard and bumpy and very uncomfortable. Although it was only six o'clock, all Chrissy wanted to do was lie in bed.

Caroline finished combing her shiny blonde hair and perched on the side of her own bed. "I know how you must be feeling," she said. "It's terrible to be looking forward to seeing someone again and then have everything go wrong like that."

Chrissy sighed again. "It's not just making a fool of myself in front of Jeff," she said. "It's this!" She pulled back her sheet and revealed her back and legs to be approximately the color of a tomato.

"Chrissy!" Caroline said in horror. "Mama mia, are you burned."

"No kidding!"

"Well, we did warn you," Caroline said. "You thought you knew better."

"I know I did," Chrissy growled. She didn't need to be reminded.

"Would you like me to get you some ice?" Caroline asked kindly.

"I don't want anything to touch this skin, not even ice," Chrissy said. "I feel terrible, Cara. I can't lie in any position without something touching my sunburn. And I thought I'd be fine because I already had a good tan from San Francisco. I kept looking at myself and I couldn't see the burn coming. . . ."

"You never can," Caroline said. "You think you're fine and then, wham, it hits you."

"It sure does," Chrissy agreed. "This must be the worst case of sunburn anyone ever had. Do you think I have terminal sunburn?"

Caroline had to smile. "I think you'll just feel uncomfortable for a while and then you'll peel," she said.

"Oh, no," Chrissy wailed. "Now I know I'm doomed where Jeff is concerned! How will he ever love me if I'm all blotchy and peeling?

Yuck!" She turned on her side, groaning, then propped herself up on one elbow so that she could face Caroline. "I should have listened to you and had the guts to go straight up to him. Maybe we'd be walking happily down the beach together by now if I'd done that. Instead, everything's ruined. I'll never see him again—I know it."

"Sure you will, Chrissy," Caroline consoled. "I bet he'll be happy to know it was all a misunderstanding."

"But I can't move, Cara," Chrissy said. "Every bit of me hurts. I won't get a chance to explain to him, ever. And I won't be able to wear clothes again for days."

Caroline grinned again. "So?" she asked. "Maybe you've just come up with a way to get his interest back."

"Very funny." Chrissy scowled at her. She turned onto her stomach again, her voice partially muffled by the pillow. "I don't think you realize how bad I feel. This is the end of everything," she said. "I might just as well stop breathing now."

Caroline got up and stared at her cousin, making Chrissy feel even more uncomfortable. "Why is life always so dramatic with you?" she asked. "Every situation you are involved in turns into a major soap opera."

"It does not," Chrissy objected. "I just have the ups and downs of a normal teenager."

"Ha!"

"I've never crashed a plane in a snowstorm and fallen madly in love while stranded in an empty house like a certain someone I know," Chrissy said pointedly, lifting her face an inch from the pillow. "I've never done anything as dramatic as that. . . ." She let her face fall back with a huge sigh. "Nope, this is just about as dramatic as I get." She shifted her position on the cot and grimaced in pain.

Caroline went over and put a hand gently on her cousin's back. Although the pressure of Caroline's hand was slight, it was enough to make Chrissy wince. Quickly Caroline drew her hand back. "Wow—you really are burning up," she said. "This looks serious, Chrissy. Maybe I should ask Tracy's aunt to take a look at it and see if you need a doctor."

"No, don't do that," Chrissy said. "I don't want Tracy's aunt to worry. Besides, she might know of some ancient Hawaiian remedy for sunburn. She might make me rub on monkeys' feet and swallow a broth of vultures' gizzards and lizards' claws!"

"She's not one of the witches from Macbeth!" Caroline said, giggling. "And how do you know one of her remedies wouldn't work? Some herbal medicines are very effective, Chrissy."

"I'd rather spray on Solarcaine," Chrissy said. "That comes in a clearly marked can containing no monkeys' feet."

Caroline headed toward the door. "I'll go buy

you some if it will make you feel better," she offered.

"Thanks, Cara," Chrissy said. "I have a feeling it's going to be a long two weeks."

"Do you want me to bring you some ice cream, too? Rocky road maybe?" Caroline asked.

Chrissy gave another huge sigh. "No, thanks. I don't feel like eating anything. I think maybe my stomach is sunburned inside as well as outside."

Caroline closed the door quietly behind her and Chrissy fell back onto her pillow with a groan. *Why did I have to come to Hawaii?* she thought. *I knew I should have gone straight home to my folks. Caroline was right when she said no good ever comes of chasing a guy.*

She had drifted into an uneasy sleep when Caroline came back again. She awoke with a start at the sound of the door opening and saw that it was already evening. The gray twilight seemed to amplify the street sounds from outside—the honking of car horns, the screech of brakes, a burst of singing from a radio. Chrissy lifted her head carefully.

"How are you feeling now?" Caroline asked, sitting down beside her. Tracy stood one step behind with a very worried look on her face.

"I know that I don't want to come back as a lobster in my next life," Chrissy answered.

"My aunt is worried about you," Tracy said. "She wants to know if you need a doctor."

"I just want to lie here," Chrissy said. "That's all I want to do."

"Shall we bring you some dinner?" Tracy asked, looking worried.

"I'm not hungry," Chrissy muttered.

"You want a drink of iced lemonade?"

"I'm not thirsty."

"So are you just going to lie there for the next two weeks?" Tracy asked.

"Uh-huh."

Caroline got out the can of sunburn medication and sprayed it onto Chrissy's back. Chrissy suffered with no more than a gasp, then lay back again, groaning.

"Oh, by the way," Caroline said as she sprayed Chrissy's thigh. "I just happened to pop into the Banyan Court on my way back."

"You did? Was Jeff there?"

"Yup."

"Did you speak to him?"

"I couldn't. It was too crowded."

"I see."

There was a silence.

"So why are you telling me this?" Chrissy asked at last.

"I thought I might put in a good word for you," Caroline said, "but it turned out it was too awkward."

"Too crowded, you mean?"

"No—there was this girl. . . ."

"Girl? With Jeff?" Chrissy propped herself up on one elbow.

"I don't know if she was actually *with* Jeff,"

Caroline said carefully. "But she was definitely hanging around. She was standing right beside the stage, almost leaning against Jeff's drums."

"Leaning against?" Chrissy asked.

"Almost."

Another pause. "Did Jeff, er, notice her?"

"How could he fail to notice?" Caroline asked with a smile. "I mean, the girl was . . . how shall I put it? . . . well built."

"She was?"

"Very exotic. She had long black hair and one of those wrap-around dresses that hardly wrapped around anything. . . ."

"I knew it," Chrissy declared, pounding her fist onto the cot. "It's just as I thought. He's already going for another girl."

"I didn't say he was going for her. All I could see was that she was trying real hard and she was very exotic-looking. Did I mention she had a flower tucked behind her ear?"

"A flower behind her ear?" Chrissy sat up. She swung her legs onto the floor. "That does it," she said.

"Chrissy, what are you doing?" Tracy asked in horror.

"Getting dressed," Chrissy said. "I've got work to do."

Tracy looked at her as if she were nuts. "Are you sure you should be getting out of bed?"

"Are you kidding?" Chrissy asked, pulling her nightshirt over her head with exclamations of pain. "You don't think I'm letting Jeff go, do you?" she added as she slipped on her thongs and ran out into the night.

Chapter 7

Chrissy ran all the way to the Banyan Court. The pain from her clothes rubbing against her sunburned body was almost completely numbed by the picture in her mind of a sexy, dark-haired girl with a flower behind her ear just about to capture Jeff's attention. She imagined the girl leaning against his drums, smiling at him, and Jeff thinking, "Oh, what the heck? Chrissy's busy with all her surfing buddies, so . . ." then turning toward the girl with an answering smile.

When she finally reached the Banyan Court, Chrissy was hot and sticky. Her blonde hair was plastered to her cheeks and her T-shirt clung to her, but she didn't care anymore. It was now or never if she wanted to fight for Jeff. She pushed past a group of tourists coming out of the hotel and went inside.

She could hear The Earthquakes playing their tribute to Elvis. Brian, their lead guitarist, was crooning, "Love me tender, love me true," into the microphone while Jeff backed it up with a heavy bass beat and brushes on the cymbals. Chrissy squeezed into the back of the court, peering around a thick clump of arial roots of the banyan tree to watch the stage. From her position in the dark corner, Chrissy felt hidden from Jeff's view so she could watch him safely. There was no sultry girl leaning against Jeff right now. Instead, he looked cool in his white Mexican shirt and very relaxed as he played.

He turned his head slightly as he reached for the cymbals and the spotlight caught his blond hair, flying about as he shook his head to the beat. He was smiling now, the spotlight flashing on his perfect teeth. He was even more gorgeous than the picture of him that she carried around in her mind. She experienced the same pounding heart that she felt the first time she had glimpsed him. It was pure torture to be so near him, to watch him relaxed at his drums as if he hadn't a care in the world.

He's forgotten about me already, Chrissy thought miserably. *I'll bet he's already asked the girl with the flower for a date and she's waiting for him backstage right now.*

"Love me tender, love me true, never let me go," sang the guitarist into the microphone. The room throbbed to the beat of Jeff's drums as if it were the heartbeat of the room itself. Chrissy could feel her own heart beating with overwhelming emotion. To be standing so close to Jeff and to know that she might have already lost him was almost more than she could bear. She wanted to climb up to the roof of the hut in the banyan tree and yell, "Here I am, Jeff. I love you!"

Instead, she stared at him, over the heads of the people at the tables, through the backs of the people who were dancing, her eyes boring through the darkness as if she was willing him to sense her presence and notice her. Then miraculously it happened. Chrissy could see Jeff's eyes move slowly around the room. He still appeared relaxed and at ease, with that hint of a smile playing on his lips as his gaze swept past the trunk of the big banyan. Chrissy stepped forward out of the corner. The time was right—she wanted him to see her. At first it seemed that his gaze had missed her, but then she saw him open his eyes wide in surprise as they met hers from across the room.

He's seen me, she thought, her heart beating twice as fast. *He knows I'm here.*

Then his gaze continued to move on, his hands never missing a beat on the drums. She wondered whether she had imagined it after all. The song finished to polite applause and Jeff leaned across to say something to the singer.

Brian nodded and picked up the microphone.

"We're going to be taking a short break, ladies and gentlemen," he said, "but we'll be back soon with more oldies and goodies. If you have a personal favorite, let us know as we continue our salute to the fifties and sixties."

The audience broke into murmured chatter and the lights rose. Chrissy stood rooted to the spot as she watched Jeff get up and walk across to her. As he came closer she expected his face to break into a big smile. Instead, his worried frown increased.

"Chrissy?" he asked in an uncertain voice. "Are you in some sort of trouble?"

"Trouble, no, why?"

"You look terrible."

"Gee, thanks, you sure know how to flatter a girl!" Chrissy exclaimed, folding her arms across her chest.

Jeff looked her up and down critically. "Well, look at you, Chrissy. Your face is bright red and you're plastered with sweat. You sure none of your surfer friends have been giving you trouble?"

"Yes, I'm fine." Chrissy said impatiently.

"Oh, that's good." He reached out to touch her shoulder.

Instinctively, she stepped away from him to protect her sunburn.

His eyes narrowed. "Fine." He turned away.

"No, you don't understand," Chrissy said rapidly. "I have really bad sunburn on my shoulders."

"I see," Jeff said, but it didn't sound as if he

understood. He looked around uneasily. "Well, I guess I'd better get back to the band. They don't pay us to take breaks."

"Jeff," Chrissy pleaded. "I came down to see you, to explain about this morning. . . ."

"You don't have to explain to me. You looked like you were having a great time. I don't want to get in your way."

"But what I said was true," Chrissy said. "Those guys were giving me my first surfing lesson. I'd just met them on the beach. They were just being friendly and I fell off a surfboard and I screamed and this guy caught me. That's why he had his arms around me. . . ."

"It's okay, Chrissy," Jeff cut in. "It's none of my business what you do."

"But, Jeff!" Chrissy insisted. "Don't you understand. I came to Hawaii to see you."

There was a pause. Above them the lights in the banyan tree began to blink on and off.

"You did?"

Chrissy looked at him solemnly and nodded.

Is he pleased to see me? Chrissy asked herself, desperately searching his eyes for a clue to his feelings. *Why doesn't he fling his arms around me and tell me how much he was missing me? That's what I feel like doing to him.*

"That's a lot of money to spend to see me," he said at last.

"It wasn't too bad," Chrissy said. "You know my friend Tracy, well we're staying with her aunt. It just seemed too good to turn down."

Jeff nodded again.

"We just arrived last night," Chrissy went on, unnerved by his silence. "You're not mad at me, are you? I got this invitation to come and I thought that . . ."

"Of course I'm not mad," Jeff said hastily.

"I couldn't tell. You aren't exactly dancing with joy."

"Chrissy," he said and reached out a hand, thought better of it, then lowered it again. "It's just a shock, that's all. I wasn't expecting to see you here. When I saw you in the surf I thought it was a dream. I still can't get over the fact that you are actually here."

"I guess you've been pretty busy," Chrissy blurted out, "with the girl who wears the flower behind her ear."

"The what?"

Chrissy gave him an odd look. That wasn't like Jeff to forget a good-looking girl. "The well-built, sexy girl, remember? Caroline saw her leaning all over your drums."

"First I've heard about it," Jeff said. "Believe me, if a sexy girl with a flower behind her ear leaned over my drums, I'd remember it. You say Caroline saw her?"

Chrissy nodded. "Yeah, earlier this evening."

Jeff smiled. "If I didn't know Caroline, I'd say she was dreaming."

"Or maybe inventing the whole thing?" Chrissy said sweetly.

"Nah, Caroline wouldn't do a thing like that."

"Of course not," Chrissy said.

There was another pause.

"So you're over here in Hawaii?" Jeff said as if he was still digesting the fact. "For how long?"

"Two weeks," Chrissy said softly.

Jeff's eyes held hers. "Two whole weeks?" he echoed. "Where are you staying?"

"Three blocks away from here," Chrissy answered. "And I guess I'd better be getting back because I ran out without telling anyone where I was going."

"That's great," Jeff said with a big smile. "Hey, Chrissy, that's fantastic."

"It is?" Chrissy said happily.

"I'm sharing a condo with two other guys just up by the canal."

"That's where I am."

"Terrific." Chrissy could tell now that he was very glad to see her, and she felt that her heart would burst with happiness. From the background came sounds of a guitar tuning up. Jeff glanced in that direction. "Look, I have to get back to work now or I'm in big trouble," he said. "Can you stick around a while? I get off at eleven tonight."

"I really should go back, I guess," Chrissy said slowly. "Tracy's aunt is supposed to be really strict and old-fashioned. I think she only invited us along so we could keep an eye on Tracy."

"But it's not even nine yet," Jeff said, astonished. "Do you mean you have to file a flight plan before nine o'clock?"

Chrissy grinned awkwardly. "I'm sure it will be fine once we've been here a bit longer," she said. "It's just that I ran out without telling them tonight."

"Why did you do that?"

"Because I . . . er . . . no reason. I just wanted to set everything straight with you as soon as possible," she said.

Jeff smiled at her and went to slide an arm around her shoulders. Then he drew it back quickly. "Sorry, I keep forgetting about your sunburn," he said. "I sure hope it goes away soon. Do you know how hard it is to keep from touching you?"

They had walked as far as the hotel foyer where large potted palms grew on either side of the doorway. Chrissy looked at Jeff and smiled shyly. "I didn't burn my lips too badly," she said.

Jeff put one finger under her chin and drew her toward him. "That's good," he said, kissing her gently at first, then more demandingly. As he kissed her, he wrapped his hands around her shoulders.

"Ow!" she exclaimed, breaking away.

Jeff grinned. "Sorry. I got carried away," he said. "In fact, it's a good thing for both of us that I'm working tonight, because I find it very hard to keep my hands to myself when you are around. You go home and take care of that sunburn, okay?"

"Okay," Chrissy said happily. "Will I see you in the morning?"

Jeff looked up toward the stage, where the band seemed just about ready to start playing. "Hold on a minute. I'll tell them to start without me," he said, "then I'll walk you part of the way home and we can talk."

"I don't want to get you in trouble," Chrissy said.

"Nah, they can do a few more oldies and goodies that don't really need the drums," Jeff said easily. "It's no big deal." He turned and disappeared into the darkness.

Chrissy watched him go with a big happy smile on her face. Everything had turned out just as she had dreamed. *What a complete dummy I was*, she thought. *Now I've wasted a whole day I could have spent with Jeff plus I've ended up with the worst case of sunburn ever. I sure hope it goes away quickly. I'll even try one of Aunt Hattie's remedies, if it will clear up this sunburn in a hurry!*

At that moment Jeff appeared again, smiling confidently as he slipped his hand into hers. It felt so wonderful to have that warm, secure hand holding hers tightly. Chrissy beamed happily at him. "Was there any problem with your escaping?"

"Of course not," he said. "They weren't very happy at first, but I think they understood when I explained that I met you."

They stepped out into the soft night air. Music was everywhere, mingling with the ringing of bicycle bells as pedicabs cruised past and the murmur of many voices as tourists wandered delightedly through the night markets. Chrissy felt as if she had rubbed Aladdin's lamp and gotten her wish, appearing in a wonderland, complete with handsome prince, in which she could live happily ever after. It seemed as if her feet were not even touching the ground as she floated along beside Jeff, feeling the warmth of his hand sending a tingle all the way up her arm.

They turned from the noisy main street into a tree-lined residential block. Here it was quiet and dark and the air was sweet with the scent of hundreds of flowers in bloom. Jeff's hand squeezed Chrissy's fingers harder.

"I'm very glad you are here," he said in a low voice. "It's going to be just perfect—just you and me and nobody else."

"That sounds like heaven, Jeff," Chrissy said with a contented sigh.

"This is a once-in-a-lifetime opportunity for us," Jeff told her. "Do you realize that I am sharing a condo with two other guys? No parents within a couple of thousand miles. We've never had a real chance to be alone before, have we? But now . . ." He let the sentence trail off as he took both of Chrissy's hands in his and pulled her very close to him.

"Except for two roommates at your condo," Chrissy reminded him, trying to sound light and unconcerned.

"My roommates both have girlfriends here," Jeff whispered, his blue eyes looking steadily into hers, "so they're not always home at night. It couldn't be better. No more quick good-night kisses in the car." He nuzzled at her ear and Chrissy drew away in confusion. Jeff misinterpreted her movement.

"But first you have to get rid of that crazy sunburn," he said firmly. "Do whatever you have to—I don't want to waste a minute of this precious time, do you?"

"Of course I don't," she said, but inside she didn't feel as confident as she sounded. She looked around. "You ought to get back to your band or you might be here without a job," she added casually.

"You're right. I guess I should be going," Jeff said. "Can you get home okay from here?"

"Oh, sure. It's only up a couple of blocks."

"I'll call you in the morning," Jeff said. "What's your phone number?"

Chrissy shook her head. "I didn't think to learn it."

"And I don't know mine, either," he said, laughing. "What about your address?"

Chrissy looked embarrassed. "I know where it is," she said, "but I don't know the street number. It's a big white apartment building. You can't miss it. . . ."

Jeff laughed. "Oh, sure," he said. "Do you know how many big white apartment buildings there are in Waikiki? Tell you what—I'll meet you at the Banyan Court tomorrow at noon, okay? None of us gets up much before that."

"Sure. Tomorrow at noon. That will be fine."

"I'll be waiting impatiently," Jeff said in a husky voice. He took her shoulders very gently and pulled her close to him. His lips came to meet hers in a warm, lingering kiss that left her feeling breathless and lightheaded.

"Go work on getting rid of that sunburn," he whispered as he finally let her go. Then he turned and hurried back toward the lights of the hotel.

Chapter 8

"Hold on there, little lady. Slow down!" Wilfred the doorman called as Chrissy pushed open the big double glass doors of the apartment complex. He moved with surprising grace for his size to hold the door open for her. "You look hotter than a roast pig at a luau," he continued in his deep, rumbling voice, the rumble of words turning into a laugh like a volcano about to erupt. "You have to learn to take things easy," he continued. "On these islands we never rush. You start running around and you're going to drop dead with heat stroke before you know where you are."

"Sorry," Chrissy apologized. She didn't want to be rude, but she had to get back to the apartment.

"Don't say sorry to me," he said, the rumbling

laugh resuming. "I ain't the one going to be carried out of here in a box. No, sirree. What's the big hurry, anyway?"

"I didn't want to be gone too long," Chrissy explained quickly. "I thought Aunt Hattie might start to worry about me."

Wilfred put his hands on his hips and gave Chrissy a look of confusion. "But you only just this moment went out," he said. "Ain't nobody going to start worrying about you yet."

Chrissy glanced down at her watch and saw that it was true. She had only been away from the apartment for half an hour! So much had happened in that half hour that she felt as if she must have been away for hours.

"I can't believe I was only gone such a short while," she said, looking up at Wilfred's big smiling face with amazement. In that short time away she had gone through enough emotions for an entire mini-series! She was conscious of Wilfred still looking at her as though she'd lost a few marbles. "I'd better be getting along now," she said. "Thank you, Wilfred."

She could still hear his rumbling laugh long after she turned the corner to the Wongs' apartment.

"Oh, Chrissy, you're back!" Tracy said with relief, opening the door to let her in. They headed down the hall toward the bedroom. "We were worried when you left in such a hurry! My aunt thought you went out to buy more sunburn medication, but Caroline was sure you'd gone to find Jeff. I don't know what gave her that idea."

"Is your aunt mad at me for going out alone?" Chrissy asked cautiously.

"She was just worried when you went running out of the apartment like that. I told her that you were always weird and not to worry," Tracy finished with a grin. "So where did you go?"

Chrissy looked down at her hands. "I went to see Jeff," she said.

"But ten minutes before you were lying there saying you wanted to die," Tracy insisted. "What brought about this miraculous cure?"

"The medication Cara brought back with her," Chrissy said, giving Caroline a long hard stare as she entered the bedroom to find her cousin waiting for her. Caroline stared straight back at Chrissy without blinking an eye.

"And did the medication work?" she asked Chrissy innocently.

Chrissy sat gingerly on the edge of the cot and nodded. "Better than you can ever guess," she said.

"So you saw Jeff?" Tracy demanded. "Tell us all about it. Did you manage to explain things to him?"

Chrissy nodded again.

"And he understood okay?"

"Oh, yes."

"And now everything is wonderful again?" Caroline asked cautiously.

Chrissy nodded again.

"So will you stop waggling your head up and

down? You remind me of Woody Woodpecker," Caroline remarked.

"I don't know what to say," Chrissy said simply. "I saw Jeff and he understood and I guess everything is great."

"Chrissy, I'm so glad for you," Tracy exclaimed. "I just knew it would be fine. Now I suppose we'll hardly see you for the next two weeks, and even when we do you'll be off in your own little dreamland."

"I guess so," Chrissy replied, but she was too confused to show any enthusiasm.

Caroline looked at her for a moment. "Are you feeling okay?" she asked. "Maybe you should lie down. You might be feeling queasy from the sun."

"I do feel strange," Chrissy admitted.

"Maybe you need some food," Caroline suggested.

"Not really . . . I'm still not hungry."

"Well, I think you need food," Caroline insisted. She turned toward Tracy. "Why don't you bring her some of that dessert your aunt made? It was so delicious, I know she'll feel like eating that."

"Good idea," Tracy agreed, then she disappeared into the hallway, leaving Chrissy and Caroline alone.

"You made the whole thing up, didn't you?" Chrissy asked as she bent to take off her sandals.

"Made what up?"

"The girl with the flower. There was no such person."

Caroline gave a mysterious smile. "I might have

been mistaken," she said. "She might have been interested in one of the other guys in the band."

"And *you're* the one who tells *me* not to interfere in other people's lives," Chrissy reminded her cousin.

"I was worried about you," Caroline defended herself. "It wasn't like you to give up. I thought if I could just make you mad enough ... it did work, didn't it? I got you back with Jeff."

"Oh, it worked just fine," Chrissy said, pulling off her T-shirt and grabbing for the can of Solarcaine once more.

"And everything's just great and perfect and wonderful, just like you thought it would be?" Caroline asked. Chrissy looked up at the questioning tone in her voice.

"Of course it is. Why shouldn't it be?"

"No reason. Only . . ."

"Only what?"

"Only I know you pretty well by now," Caroline said slowly, "and I know that when Chrissy Madden is on top of the world, like she says she is now, the rest of the world knows about it. She yells and sings and does crazy dances and acts like your basic nut case. But tonight you are very quiet." Caroline lowered her voice and looked at Chrissy in concern. "So I just wondered if something had not gone right after all."

Chrissy looked up and smiled. "You do know me well," she said.

"So wasn't he happy to see you?"

"He was delighted. He kept on saying how

wonderful it was and what a great time we'd have together."

"Sounds good to me," Caroline said. "So what's bugging you? You're not as pleased to see him as you thought you'd be?"

"I am, Cara. I thought my heart would pound right out of my chest when he walked across the room to me. It's just that . . . I don't know. Maybe I'm being childish."

She looked up as Tracy's footsteps clattered down the hall.

"What's up?" Caroline asked, glancing toward the doorway. "Don't you want Tracy to know about this?"

Chrissy shook her head and pretended to zip her lips. "So I guess I won't be staying out in the sun much any more," she said brightly, as the door opened.

Tracy brought a tray over to Chrissy's bed. "How does this tempt your appetite?" she asked, presenting Chrissy with a pineapple boat filled with ice cream. "Look, the boat's even got a banana funnel. When we were little my aunt used to put spirits into the banana and lit it so the funnel smoked. We thought it was magic!"

"It looks pretty magical to me without the smoke," Chrissy said. "In fact, I suddenly find that I'm hungry after all. So if you ladies will excuse me?" She began to attack the ice cream, giving a deep sigh of contentment as she swallowed the first spoonful.

"We won't be mean enough to sit around and

watch you eat like a pig," Tracy said, laughing. "We'll see you in a while. I should help my aunt with the dishes, anyway." She turned to leave. Caroline got up to go also.

"You said you were going to finish spraying the Solarcaine on my back for me, Cara," Chrissy said as Caroline reached the door.

"Oh, sure. Which parts didn't we do?" she asked. "Be right with you, Tracy."

They both waited until Tracy's footsteps died away.

"Was that mean of me to get rid of Tracy?" Chrissy asked. "I just didn't feel like talking about it in front of her. She's such a great friend, but . . ."

"I understand, Chrissy. This is cousin talk, right?" Caroline asked with a reassuring smile. "So what happened tonight that has made you so nervous?"

"Am I nervous?" Chrissy asked. "I didn't think I was, just confused."

"And nervous, too," Caroline said firmly. "You can't keep still. You've been bouncing your leg up and down and fiddling with your hair. It's obvious—to me, anyway."

Chrissy realized that Caroline was right. She dropped the strand of hair that she'd been winding around her finger and forced her leg still.

"So I guess I am nervous," she admitted. "Maybe I'm just overreacting. I don't know."

"About what?"

"Jeff was really glad to see me," Chrissy said,

"and that was great, except he kept dropping hints about the condo he's sharing and how ideal it is and how his roommates are out lots of nights, so we'll be able to have the place to ourselves."

There was a pause.

"I see," Caroline said. "And you think they were definitely hints?"

"No doubt about it," Chrissy said. "I'm not totally naive, Cara. I might have led a sheltered life back in Iowa, but I could tell by the way he looked at me—he was thinking Sex with a capital S!"

"I don't think you need to look so worried," Caroline said gently. "I mean, Jeff's a nice guy. If he really cares about you, he wouldn't pressure you into something you didn't want. Just tell him you're not ready for that sort of commitment yet, if that's how you feel."

Chrissy put her empty dish on the tray with a clang. "I don't know what I feel, Cara. That's part of the problem. You know what I think about Jeff! I think the sun shines out of his head. I don't want to lose him, Cara, but I don't know what I should do. I'm a little hick from the boonies and he's a sophisticated city boy."

"Love is love wherever you go," Caroline said. "Where you live doesn't change the way two people feel about each other. You have to behave how you feel is right, Chrissy."

"But I'm not sure," Chrissy said with a big sigh. "I mean, why am I so worried about being alone with him at his condo? Don't you think I should be learning to act more mature and sophisticated by now?"

"Not if doing what you think is mature and sophisticated is also wrong in your mind," Caroline said firmly. "You have to act the way that feels right to you, Chrissy. Not because your family or boyfriend expects it of you. The only one you should be listening to is your own conscience, because you are the person you've got to live with."

"But what if I'm just behind the times because I don't know any better? Jeff seems to think it's only natural that we should spend the night together at his place." She twirled a lock of hair around her finger and looked at her cousin with worried eyes. "Cara, I don't think I'm ready, but I don't want him to think I'm a weirdo."

"You're not a weirdo. You're just a normal girl with normal doubts," Caroline said. "You're going through what every other girl on the planet goes through."

"You mean, it's not only us girls from Iowa who have this problem?" Chrissy asked, only half-jokingly.

Caroline laughed. "Do you think we grow up knowing about boys and sex in San Francisco? We're all just as confused. At least, I know I am."

"I get the feeling that most girls around school are pretty experienced by the time they get to senior year," Chrissy said.

"I don't think so," Caroline disagreed. "I know some kids may have decided that sex is okay for them, but most of them have decided that it's definitely better to wait."

"And what do you think, Cara?" Chrissy asked quietly.

"I haven't had to make that decision yet," Caroline said hesitantly, her cheeks turning red, "so I can't really judge what I'd do. That's the problem. Nobody else can judge for you, Chrissy. All I can say is: don't ever do anything you'd regret, especially not just to please a boy! If he really loves you, he'll understand, and if he doesn't really love you, well then you're better off without him."

Chrissy thought about her cousin's advice. "You're right, Cara," she declared. "I'm glad you're here. It's a good thing one of us has her head on straight. I really don't feel ready to spend the night with a boy in a condo, even if that boy is Jeff. I know I'd feel bad about it afterwards."

"There you are," Caroline said, reaching out to pat Chrissy's shoulder. "Whoops, sorry," she said, drawing her hand back. "Nearly forgot the sunburn. As I was saying, just talking things through with someone else always helps."

Chrissy laughed nervously. "Now all I have to do is convince Jeff of the way I feel. Maybe I'd better go lie in the sun some more tomorrow. . . ."

"Chrissy! You're already badly burned!" Caroline reminded her.

"That's what I mean! I'll have to keep up the sunburn for two weeks so he's not allowed to touch me." She began to giggle. "Oh, Cara," she wailed, "why is life so darned complicated? I'm crazy about Jeff, and his kisses are absolutely . . ." She paused for a moment to think. "Well, his kisses are just so wonderful, there's no word for it! But do I have to stop him from kissing me now because I don't want to give him ideas? Whoever invented boys should have included instructions!"

Caroline started to laugh, too. "That's for sure. But aren't you glad they were invented?"

"Are you kidding? Boys are my main hobby in life!" Chrissy answered with a grin, but then her expression turned serious. "I do hope I don't spoil everything with Jeff. He'll understand, won't he?"

"I hope so, Chrissy," Caroline said. "I hope you have a wonderful time here with him that you remember for the rest of your life. Only don't get carried away," she cautioned. "And don't go lying out in the sun for hours again, please! I can feel the heat from your skin making the whole room warm."

"Don't worry, I've learned my lesson. Physics lesson number one: the sun is hot. It burns, especially backs and legs. Which reminds me— you never did finish spraying my back for me. Right down here, where it's sort of tomato colored."

Caroline picked up the can and giggled as Chrissy let out a shriek of horror.

"Cara, that stuff is cold!" Chrissy yelled.

"I know, it's supposed to be. Now sit still," Caroline ordered. "There," she said at last. "You are all covered in pain-killer. Now do you feel like being sociable and joining everyone in the living room?"

"Sure," Chrissy said. "Hey, Cara, thanks for the talk. I feel much better now. I'm sure everything will be just fine when I explain to Jeff how I feel," she added, but inside she still wasn't so sure.

Chapter 9

The next day Chrissy spent the whole morning sitting in the shade, draped in a long-sleeved blouse, a big straw hat, and loads of towels covering her legs. She sat by herself, watching Caroline and Tracy splashing in the water, and watching the boys show off their surfing skills. During that long morning, all she thought about was Jeff and his darned condo, so that by the time she met him at noon she was as tense as the strings on a guitar.

"How's the famous sunburn?" he asked, grinning happily as he greeted her outside the Banyan Court. He gently lifted her collar away from her neck and whistled softly. "Phew. You could cook an egg on that. You must be hurting bad."

"I didn't manage to sleep too much last night," Chrissy said and instantly bit her tongue. Why did she have to launch straight into subjects like that! "I mean, it was impossible to find an unburned part of me to lie on," she said hastily, glad for once that sunburn did hide her embarrassed cheeks.

Jeff was still smiling easily. "I'm going to make very sure that I keep you out of the sun for the next few days," he said.

Now what does he mean by that? she asked herself.

"You might find yourself in pretty bad shape if you add to that burn," he said, his face becoming suddenly serious. "So what do you want to do? You want to come back to my condo?"

"Come back to your condo?" Why did it have to come out as a squeak?

"I thought you might like to meet my roommates. They are really nice guys, and since we can't go to the beach until your sunburn goes away . . ."

"We could wander around the stores," Chrissy suggested.

Jeff made a face. "You know what I think about shopping," he said. "Besides, everything here is so gimmicky. Come on," he said and took her hand, "we'll go back to my place and have some lunch and then I can play you the demo tape my group did. I think it sounds pretty good. You'll be the first person outside the group to hear it!"

"Okay," Chrissy said reluctantly.

They turned off the main street and walked back in the shade of flowering trees.

"You're very quiet," Jeff said. "Are you sure you're not a Chrissy clone? The Chrissy I knew back in San Francisco could never shut up for more than two seconds."

"I guess it's the sunburn," Chrissy said.

Jeff laughed. "You sunburned your tongue? I don't believe it. You told me yesterday that you didn't sunburn your lips, remember?"

"I remember," Chrissy mumbled. *Rats, why did I have to say that last night!* she thought.

"You're not still thinking about those guys on the beach?" Jeff asked. He said it teasingly, but Chrissy sensed an undercurrent of seriousness in his voice.

"Of course not," she answered. "I told you, I only met them yesterday morning. They're all with Caroline and Tracy at the beach right now."

Jeff nodded. "I hope you didn't get in trouble for staying out last night."

"No, but they were wondering where I'd gone," Chrissy answered. She glanced across at him quickly, to find him gazing at her with a look of concern in his eyes. He reached out and took Chrissy's hand, squeezing it tightly in his. *He is such a nice guy,* she thought, glancing across at him through her hair. *I'm getting uptight over nothing.*

They reached the canal, which stretched, blue and shimmering, along a bright green golf course. In the background the mountains rose into the clouds, to create an atmosphere of brooding and mystery.

"Here we are," Jeff announced. "Not very fancy but cheap!" He led her into a complex of two-story wooden buildings, facing a central parking area. Each building had a thatched balcony and a small grove of coconut palms, making them look exotic, despite the peeling paint. Jeff led her across the parking lot and up a flight of steps running up the outside of the building. On the balcony he paused and dug into his pocket for the key.

"Now where did I put it this time?" he asked. He rang the doorbell instead. "I hope my roommates are home to let us in."

Chrissy paused at the edge of the balcony. Was this all a plot after all? Had he arranged with his roommates not to be home? "Well, what do you know?" he'd say. "We have the place to ourselves after all! Surprise, surprise!"

At last someone opened the door just wide enough to peek out.

"Oh, it's you!" a voice growled. "Why did you have to wake us up?"

"Sorry, guys, I must have forgotten my key again," Jeff said.

The door opened wider to reveal a tall, lanky

boy in T-shirt and surfer shorts. He blinked blearily from the light. "We thought you might be the landlord coming to complain about last night's party," he said.

"I've brought Chrissy back to meet you guys," Jeff said, turning to take her hand. "You'd better go tell Wayne to make himself decent."

The lanky guy peered at Chrissy, then shuffled back into the apartment, while Chrissy followed Jeff cautiously into a dark living room.

When her eyes had adjusted to the light, she could see that the room was an absolute mess. Clothes were all over the floor, along with newspapers, guitars, and fried-chicken boxes. The table was piled high with dirty plates and glasses and in the kitchen area at the far end of the room she spotted a leaning tower of pots and pans in the sink.

"Holy cow, what a mess!" Chrissy said before she could stop herself.

"The guys had a party last night," Jeff said. "They cooked spaghetti."

"I can see that. There's some stuck to the ceiling," Chrissy commented.

Jeff grinned. "They heard that was the way to tell if it was cooked." He picked a pile of newspapers off the vinyl sofa. "Here, sit down. I'll see if there's a soft drink in the fridge."

"Are you kidding?" Chrissy asked, her nerves restored by the sight of the incredible chaos. Normally she was a slob herself, but not nearly as bad as this! "How can you guys live in a pigsty like this? It's disgusting."

She began to carry dirty plates across to the kitchen and to attack the mountain of dishes. Jeff followed her, halfheartedly handing her more items to wash. They had almost finished when Jeff's roommates reappeared in fresh clothes and with neatly combed hair. They stopped in delight when they saw the improvement in the messy apartment.

"Hey, who is the miracle worker?" asked the husky dark-haired boy.

"This is Chrissy," Jeff said. "I brought her here to clean up after you guys."

"That was the only reason, right?" the boy asked with a grin.

"Cut it out, guys. This is Chrissy! Remember, I told you about her? We knew each other back in San Francisco."

Why not say we were going together back in San Francisco? Chrissy thought fleetingly as she smiled politely.

"This is Wayne," Jeff said, pointing at the boy who had spoken, "and this creep who almost didn't let us in is Carl. Wayne plays the drums, too, with a group at the Tidal Wave nightclub and Carl plays the keyboard," Jeff added.

"So what are you doing here?" Wayne asked Chrissy.

"On vacation," she said.

"You could have told us that you were coming here this afternoon, Jeff," Carl said. "We could have beat it for you."

"It's okay," Jeff said. "I wanted Chrissy to meet you guys."

"I can't think why, unless she likes horror movies," Wayne said. "Especially him," he added, pointing to Carl. "He's enough to give anyone the creeps."

"Look who's talking," Carl retorted.

Jeff gave Chrissy a grin. "Do you want some lunch?" he asked, opening the refrigerator door. "Hey, what happened to that stuff from the deli?" he demanded.

"We ate it, what else?" Carl said, laughing.

"You guys, the food in here is for all of us, not just you two pigs," Jeff complained. "Now I'll have to go out for Chinese food again."

"And we better get downtown. We're supposed to be meeting Marty for a practice session," Wayne said. "Come on, creep. See you guys. Nice meeting you, Chrissy. Maybe we'll see you again."

Chrissy finished tidying up the living room while Jeff disappeared down to the corner Chinese take-out restaurant. She still could not shake off the feeling of uneasiness. Maybe it was the strangeness of seeing Jeff in new surroundings with new people. Even his roommates made her uneasy. They were only throwing insults about the way her brothers and friends did at home, but somehow their insults sounded sinister today, as if every one carried a hidden meaning. She jumped as Jeff closed the front door behind him.

"Peace at last, huh?"

Chrissy nodded.

"Don't take those guys too seriously," he said as if he could read her thoughts. "They are pretty nice when you get to know them. Wayne is really great on the drums. Better than me—if that's possible!" And he gave a sudden boyish smile that made her relax again.

This is just Jeff, she thought. *This is the boy I came to Hawaii to be with.*

He took two plates from the draining board and began to divide the food from the cartons. "I hope you like sweet and sour," he said, "because there wasn't much choice: sweet and sour shrimp, sweet and sour ribs, and sweet and sour chicken."

"Fine with me," she said.

They ate with chopsticks, teasing each other over the right way to eat Chinese food. Chrissy laughed so hard when Jeff kept dropping his food that she was sorry when the meal was over and Jeff pushed the plates away.

"No, leave the washing up," he told her. "You've done more than your share today. Come and sit over on the sofa."

Chrissy moved cautiously across the room. Jeff patted the sofa beside him and slid an arm around her shoulder. Chrissy gave an exaggerated gasp of pain as he touched her.

"Still hurting pretty bad?"

"It really kills," she said, grimacing to emphasize her point.

"I'll have to remember to keep my hands to myself then." He got up from the sofa. "I've just remembered I want to show you something."

Chrissy waited, tense and curious as he crossed the room. *What is wrong with you?* she asked herself. *You have dreamed and dreamed of being with Jeff again and now that you're together, you are as jumpy as a nervous chicken on market day. This is Jeff you are with, not some strange guy you don't know!*

He put a tape into the player and came back to join her. "This is the tape I told you about," he said. "The one we just made. Our manager is going to send it to some big promoters when we get back stateside."

The music started. It was too loud for conversation, but it had a good beat. Jeff sank down beside Chrissy and gently put her head onto his shoulder. They sat there, not moving, listening to the whole tape.

When the tape finished, again there was an awkward moment of silence.

"I . . . er, guess I should be getting back to the others," Chrissy said hesitantly. "They'll wonder what's happened to me."

She expected him to protest, but instead he nodded as if he understood. "I guess your sunburn has put you under the weather," he said. "And I should be thinking about getting ready for work. We play the early shift tonight, then there's a hula show and then we play again until midnight."

"Sounds like a long evening," Chrissy commented.

"Yeah, but I'm not complaining. All that terrific money! I'll have enough to buy a new car when I get home." He paused and looked at her closely, as if he had just noticed for the first time who she really was. "It's a bummer you won't be in San Francisco when I get back," he said. "Can you imagine us zooming up and down those hills in a little sports car with the top down?"

For a moment Chrissy had a glimpse of his face, open and tender, and realized with a start that she was only now seeing the real Jeff. Until now she had felt as if she was dating a stranger. A Jeff clone—certainly not the same Jeff she'd been going out with in San Francisco.

She smiled back at him wistfully. "It would have been great," she said. "There are no hills to zoom up and down where I live—and old trucks aren't quite as fun somehow. They usually smell of chickens!"

Jeff laughed. "Come on," he said. "I'll walk you home." He leaned across and brushed her lips with his own. "That was just a down payment," he whispered, reaching out to touch her bottom lip with his finger. "And next time we get the apartment to ourselves, maybe we can make better use of it than just listening to tapes!"

The tender moment was broken for Chrissy. She managed to smile, but again she was as tense inside as the strings on a guitar. *It's like he's two people,* she thought. *One of them is a warm, funny boy who I'm crazy about and the other is only after one thing! I wish I knew which one is the real Jeff!*

Chapter 10

The sound of the drum pounded louder and
faster with every moment as six girls in traditional grass skirts ran onto the stage, their
bronzed skin glowing in the light of tiki torches.
Around their necks they wore leis of flowers
and in their long black hair perched wreaths of
green leaves. The dancers began to move to the
music, swaying slowly at first, then faster and
faster until their hips were a blur of movement
while their faces remained serene and smiling.
The audience roared its approval as the dancers
kept up the incredible pace of the hula, on and
on until it seemed to Chrissy that they would
drop from exhaustion at any moment. When
they finished they smiled shyly and bowed to
the enthusiastic applause of the audience.

Chrissy picked up her half coconut filled with iced fruit punch, and decorated with orchids and tiny paper umbrellas. It was the most exotic drink she had ever seen and it tasted even better than it looked. For once it had been worth splurging on the price.

"I'm glad you told us about the hula show, Chrissy," Tracy said. "This is great, isn't it?"

"Uh-huh," Chrissy replied. She paused with the straw in her mouth and glanced over her shoulder.

"I don't know how they manage to do that with their hips," Caroline said. "It's as if their bottom halves aren't connected to their top halves at all. Incredible!"

Tracy tapped Chrissy's elbow. "Are you looking for Jeff, Chrissy?" she asked.

"No, why?"

"You keep looking over your shoulder. I thought he went out in the other direction."

"He did," Chrissy said. "I just thought that . . . oh, forget it. I've got to try that hip-wiggling when I get back to the apartment."

"Tell your aunt to lock up the good china first!" Caroline said to Tracy with a laugh. "We all know what a disaster area Chrissy is when she tries dancing at home! Remember the time I tried to teach you some ballet steps? You not only knocked over my desk lamp, but you stomped all over my English paper."

"So I'll try it on the beach," Chrissy said with a grin. "Although somehow I don't think I'll ever mange to look as sexy as those girls."

"I think you're right about that," Caroline agreed. "That hula dance must take a lot of rehearsing, but they made it look so natural."

Tracy sighed. "Yeah, but I think I'd be a natural klutz!"

The girls stopped talking then to watch the next act. This time a tall bronzed muscleman, dressed only in a jungle-print loincloth, came out to do a fire dance. Chrissy watched him, but she wasn't really paying attention.

A cold wind seemed to come through the courtyard from the ocean, making Chrissy shiver in her light summer dress. She turned and glanced over her shoulder again. What was bothering her tonight? Did she expect to see Jeff standing in the shadows with one of those Hawaiian beauties? Hardly, she told herself. He knew she was here tonight. He wouldn't flirt with another girl in front of her. Jeff wasn't like that . . . *but something is making me uneasy,* she thought. *I don't think it's anything to do with Jeff, but I can't put my finger on it.*

The fire dancer finished to loud applause and then the dancers came back again, this time dressed in Tahitian costume, to do the Tahitian hula.

Caroline leaned toward Chrissy. "Is something the matter?" she asked. "You're really jumpy and you keep looking around."

"I don't know," Chrissy whispered back. "I've got the strangest feeling—like a prickling in my shoulder blades. I keep thinking I'm being watched. Do you think I'm paranoid?"

Caroline held her cousin with a steady gaze. "I would have thought so some other time," she said, "but I know just how you feel. When Tracy and I were out shopping earlier this afternoon, I suddenly felt like I was being followed. I didn't say anything to Tracy because it was so dumb, and then the feeling went away. But just for a few moments I didn't dare turn around or I knew I'd see something creepy."

The cousins stared at each other. "Do you think they believe in spirits and voodoo on these islands?" Chrissy asked with a nervous little laugh.

"I don't know," Caroline replied. "It's weird that both of us have felt it. Let's ask Tracy— maybe she felt it, too."

They waited until the number ended to ask Tracy, but she only laughed when Caroline put the question to her. "Have I what?" she said and giggled. "What did they put in your punch? Why would anyone follow us, anyway? We're not exactly prime targets for a mugging."

"It's nothing like that," Caroline explained. "I didn't feel in danger, just weird."

"That's just what I felt," Chrissy said. "Weird. As if something might happen at any moment."

"Maybe you two are the types that spirits go for," Tracy said, still determined to make a joke of it. "You'll be able to write your autobiography after all, Chrissy—I was the bride of the Hawaiian Volcano God!"

"Very funny, ha, ha," Chrissy said. The show had ended and she gathered up her purse.

"You're not going to hang around for Jeff tonight?" Tracy asked.

"No, I'm coming home with you guys," Chrissy said. "He doesn't get off until midnight and all this talk of spirits has made me too nervous to walk home alone."

They came from the noisy, dimly lit courtyard into the bright main street, dodging aside to avoid being run down by a speeding pedicab.

"Isn't it fun at night here?" Caroline asked, looking around excitedly. "Let's walk home through that alleyway with all the touristy stalls. I want to buy a gold charm from this guy who keeps knocking down the price each time he sees me. Besides, there are so many people, nothing can happen."

They began to walk down the crowded alleyway, lingering by each new delight, agonizing over whether they wanted four shell necklaces for five dollars, or three silver dolphins for four.

"I vote we made a list of all the things we want and then buy them on the last day," Tracy suggested. "Otherwise, we might find ourselves in mid-vacation with no money."

"Good idea," Chrissy said. "So there's no point in hanging around any longer tonight, is there? I'm kind of tired. How about you guys?"

She didn't want to say it, but the uneasiness

was growing again. She clutched her purse tightly and glanced over her shoulder. She couldn't be sure, but it looked as if a figure had just ducked behind a leather goods stall.

"Yes, let's go home now," Caroline agreed, slipping her arm through Chrissy's. "I'm suddenly tired, too."

"You're a couple of party-poopers," Tracy complained. "I didn't mean for us to go home. I just meant that we should do more window-shopping, instead of buying right away."

Caroline linked her other arm through Tracy's. "Some other time, okay? We still have a whole week and a half left to window-shop."

They started to walk purposefully through the remainder of the alleyway and came out into the complex of small shops behind it.

"Do you get the feeling we're being followed again?" Caroline whispered to Chrissy. Chrissy nodded.

"Me, too," Caroline said. "Do you think we're just imagining things?"

"I'm not sure," Chrissy said. "I thought I saw a figure move behind a stall when I turned around."

She glanced over her shoulder again. "Look," she whispered. "There is someone there. Let's hurry."

"But why would anyone choose to follow us out of all the tourists in Hawaii?" Caroline asked in a shaky voice as Chrissy dragged her forward.

"I can't see anyone," Tracy complained. "Are you two sure you're not turning cuckoo?"

But Caroline and Chrissy were already walking briskly in the direction of their apartment. Every now and then they would stop and listen, and once or twice Chrissy was sure she heard footsteps a few paces behind them.

"Surely any mugger would give up by now?" Caroline asked. "I mean, we don't look rich, do we? And we're not so wonderfully gorgeous that a guy would choose us over all those cute girls back on the main drag."

"We're almost home, thank heavens," Chrissy said as they turned the corner toward the canal. "Wilfred will know what to do!"

"I still think you girls have gone off your rockers," Tracy said. "I haven't seen anyone yet. I did hear some footsteps, but there are other people walking around Waikiki, you know."

At last they reached the front door of the building. Chrissy took one last glance down the street before they went in, but saw nothing unusual.

"Let's stand inside here and see if anyone shows up," she suggested. "We're safe now. Wilfred will deal with any muggers, won't you, Wilfred?"

"What's that, little lady? Someone been bothering you? You leave them to Wilfred!" he said, striding toward the front door as if he was going into battle. Chrissy thought any mugger would have to be pretty stupid not to run away from Wilfred.

"There's someone coming now," Wilfred said. "Two guys. Are they the ones?"

"Let's wait and see if they stop here," Caroline said, stepping back into the shadows. Her hand trembled as she grabbed Chrissy's arm, and Chrissy's heart almost stopped.

The girls heard footsteps coming nearer and nearer. They slowed down as they reached the building, then Wilfred stepped out to meet the culprits.

"Can I help you, gentlemen?" he said in his deep, rumbling voice.

"Oh, no thank you, sir," a voice said. "We were just passing by and . . ."

The two figures came into view through the glass. Suddenly Caroline let out a gleeful shout and ran forward, pushing Chrissy and Tracy aside to get through the front door.

"I don't believe it!" she gasped. Chrissy saw the boy's eyes light up and he opened his arms.

"Luke!" Caroline exclaimed. "It *is* you!" And she flung herself into his outstretched arms.

The second boy stood alone now, looking through the glass uncertainly, until his eyes met Chrissy's. He pushed a strand of blond hair out of his eyes and sauntered into the building past a puzzled Wilfred.

The boy nodded shyly. "Hi, Chrissy."

Chrissy stood as if turned to stone. "Ben," she stammered. "What on earth are you doing here?"

Chapter 11

The tall, blond-haired boy blinked again shyly and gave a little half smile. "How are you, Chrissy?" he asked. His Midwestern twang seemed out of place in exotic Waikiki.

Chrissy stared at him as if he was one of the Hawaiian spirits they had just been joking about.

"Ben Hatcher, just what are you doing here?" she demanded.

Ben looked embarrassed. "Just on a vacation, I guess," he said.

"Since when do people from Danbury, Iowa, come all the way to Hawaii for vacation?" she asked. "Did you win the church raffle or something?"

"Sort of," Ben said. "Luke won this contest on the back of a cereal box. The prize was two free trips anywhere on American Airlines, so we thought we'd like to check out Hawaii. We heard it was a real nice place to visit and a great place to pick up girls." He looked at Chrissy pointedly, but she ignored his comment.

"Was it you following us around all day?" Caroline asked Luke, leaning back in his arms to gaze up at him adoringly.

Luke nodded. "At first we were going to call you to let you know we were on our way. Then we decided to surprise you by dropping in on you here. And then . . ." he paused, then glanced at Ben, "good old Ben here came up with the brilliant idea of following you around like this. See, we wanted to give you girls a surprise you would never forget."

"I'll never forget this surprise, that's for sure," Chrissy grumbled, "but Ben, you're going to wish I would."

"Don't be such an old grouch, Chrissy," Ben told her with a mischievous grin. "I just know we're going to have one heck of a vacation here."

Before Chrissy could retort, Tracy stepped out into the street. "Would somebody mind explaining to me what is going on?" she asked. "One minute we are running from potential muggers and the next minute you fling yourselves into their arms."

Caroline turned to her friend, leaving her arm wrapped around Luke's waist. "Tracy, this is Luke!" she said simply as if that explained everything that needed to be explained in the world.

"And this is Ben," Chrissy added. "Remember, I told you about my ex-boyfriend?" She stressed the word "ex."

"This is our good friend Tracy," Caroline said, looking from Tracy's face to Luke's. "We're staying here with her aunt and uncle. Where are you guys staying?"

"We've got this little hotel right down by the beach," Luke said with a grin. "We needed something cheap and we saw it advertised at the airport. It's not bad . . ."

"If you enjoy cockroaches," Ben chimed in.

"At least they're friendly cockroaches," Luke added. "We just got in last night."

"Why don't we all go on up to the apartment," Tracy said. "We can have a cool drink and finish off that ice cream."

"Sounds like a good idea to me," Luke said. "I thought I was used to heat back home, but it sure is hot here."

"Are you coming, Chrissy?" Caroline asked.

Ben reached out and touched her arm. "Chrissy, do you think we could go for a walk instead? I'd like to talk to you alone."

Chrissy looked across at Caroline, then back at Ben and let out an exasperated sigh. "I guess that would be a good idea," she said. "We'll see you guys later."

The others disappeared into the apartment building while Chrissy turned and silently fell into step beside Ben. They crossed the wide boulevard and began to walk beside the canal. It was dark and quiet here. Only the croaking of hundreds of unseen frogs mingled with a muted roar of distant traffic.

"Okay," Chrissy said at last. "You wanted to talk to me. Talk."

"You're mad at me for showing up here, aren't you?" Ben asked.

"Of course I'm mad," Chrissy said. "Your coming here is going to spoil everything."

"With that guy Jeff, you mean?"

"How did you know about Jeff?" she asked sharply.

"You know what it's like in Danbury!" Ben said with an attempt at a laugh. "Nothing is a secret. I've been over at your folks' house for dinner when they've read your letters out loud. The name Jeff cropped up real often."

"So you didn't just come over here on a vacation?" Chrissy demanded angrily. "You knew I was here and you came over to get me back, right?"

Ben gave a short sigh. "I kept telling myself not to worry, that you'd be back home where you belong real soon, but then you wrote that you were going to Hawaii and you said that this Jeff guy would be there, too. I figured I might lose you forever if I didn't do something right away. I was even prepared to blow all my savings on the trip . . . but then Luke won the contest. It seemed like a miracle. He couldn't stop thinking about your cousin and I couldn't stop thinking about you, so we said 'What the heck,' and here we are."

"Wonderful!" Chrissy said dryly. "You sure think a lot of yourself, Ben Hatcher. Did you really expect to show up here and have me fall right back into your arms?"

"You mean the way Caroline and Luke did?" he asked. "No, Chrissy. I know I'll have to win you back, but I'll do anything to stop you from making a big fool of yourself with this Jeff."

"What do you mean, make a fool of myself?" Chrissy demanded. "I'll have you know that Jeff is a real nice guy. I love him and he loves me."

"You mean that, Chrissy? You can really look me in the eye and tell me that you two love each other the way you and I used to?"

"Sure, I can," Chrissy said, but she didn't look him in the eye.

"If that's really true, then I'll go home at the end of the week and I won't bother you again," Ben said. "I won't stand in the way of your happiness, Chrissy, because you mean more to me than all the world. But I sure as heck don't want to see you making a big mistake."

"I'm a big girl now, Ben," Chrissy said frostily. "I can take care of myself very well. Remember, I've lived in a big, sophisticated city for a whole year now. I'm not the dumb little country girl I used to be."

"I think you're still the same person deep down," Ben said. "And you've got to come back home to us soon, anyhow. You're not going to fit in very well if you walk around school with your nose ten yards in the air."

"Oh, yes, Danbury High," Chrissy said. "I'm not sure if I'll fit in well even if I don't put my nose in the air. So many things are different. I've changed my opinion about so many things and I've grown up so much, Ben."

"I've grown up, too, Chrissy," Ben said. "I haven't had an easy year. I've had to work real hard on the farm, just to keep up the payments so they don't foreclose. And the soybean crop was real poor this year and we had rust in our main silo. . . ."

None of it means anything to me anymore, Chrissy thought. *It's as if he's talking about a foreign country.* Out loud she said, "Maybe we should get back to the apartment." They turned around and headed back, an uncomfortable silence between them.

"Aren't Luke and Caroline just the most unlikely couple?" Ben asked as they neared the lights of the boulevard. "They don't seem to have a thing in common and yet just look at their faces when they are together. I guess true love like that doesn't come around too often."

"I guess not," Chrissy said uneasily.

"I used to think—" Ben began, but Chrissy cut him off.

"Please, Ben. Don't let's talk. We'll only start saying things we'll both regret later," Chrissy said, walking faster toward the apartment.

Ben followed right behind her. "Can we at least stay good friends?" he asked. "I could always count on you when I had a big problem on my mind."

"I counted on you, too," Chrissy said. "I don't see why we can't still be friends, as long as you don't start trying to run my life for me."

"I'll try real hard," Ben said. He stepped in front of Chrissy to open the apartment door.

"I just can't believe it," Caroline said for the hundredth time. "It's just like a miracle, Chrissy, isn't it?"

They were sitting out on the Wongs' balcony, enjoying the sweet night air before going to bed. Tracy was inside, talking in rusty Cantonese with her aunt and uncle. Chrissy turned her attention back from the reflection of lights in the canal.

"More like a bad dream," Chrissy said. "That was all I needed to complicate things with Jeff— to have my hick boyfriend show up here in his denim overalls!"

"So you weren't the least little bit pleased to see Ben?" Caroline asked. "You're heart didn't jump the tiniest bit when you saw him standing there?"

"I don't know!" Chrissy said irritably. "My heart jumped, but I think it was just surprise. I noticed your heart jumping all right!"

Caroline gave a huge sigh of contentment. "It was wonderful, Chrissy," she said. "It was as if we'd never been apart. The moment we were on our own we started talking as if we were finishing off yesterday's conversation. We'd both been thinking about each other nonstop since we said good-bye. Isn't that wonderful?"

"Oh, yes, wonderful," Chrissy growled. Then she got up and came across to sit on Caroline's bed. "Don't listen to me. I'm an old grouch. I'm really very happy for you, Cara. It just is kind of sickening for the rest of the world to watch two people as much in love as you are. It made me realize that . . ."

"That what?"

"Never mind," Chrissy said quickly. "So I guess I'm stuck with entertaining Ben on the beach tomorrow, whether I like it or not?"

"Oh, Chrissy, come on," Caroline said. "The guy's come halfway around the world to see you. The least you can do is show him around a little."

"And what will Jeff say if he sees me on the beach with another guy?" Chrissy asked.

"You can just explain to him that these are old friends from back home," Caroline answered simply. "Nobody could object to that, surely?"

"As long as Ben behaves like just an old friend from back home," Chrissy said. "I get the feeling he is determined to win me back from Jeff whatever happens." Chrissy paused to scratch the itchy sunburn on her back. "Cara, would you do me a gigantic favor?"

"Sure, what is it?" Caroline asked.

Chrissy looked at her cousin's happy expression and hesitated. She hadn't seen Caroline this happy since she'd met Luke back in April. But what choice did she have? She needed Caroline's help. "I know you and Luke will want to be alone together, but please don't keep going off and leaving me alone with Ben. Let's just keep it a big, friendly party, okay?"

Caroline smiled. "We'll see, Chrissy, but I want to be with Luke as much as possible," she said.

"And anyway, we don't want Tracy to feel left out of things, do we?" Chrissy asked. "After all, we are only here because she was nice enough to invite us."

"Tracy seems to be interested in that quiet guy, Jeremy," Caroline said thoughtfully. "They were actually discussing James Joyce together on the beach this afternoon, and that is doing really well for Tracy! I think she's found a kindred spirit."

"That's great," Chrissy said. "Now everybody can have a wonderful time on the beach except me. I'll have to spend every moment keeping Ben in line, and making sure that Jeff doesn't see us and get the wrong idea."

"Why don't you explain to Jeff," Caroline said, "before he gets any wrong ideas? Tell him first thing in the morning."

"I don't think so," Chrissy said. "Morning for Jeff and his buddies is anything after one o'clock, and he has a rehearsal all afternoon tomorrow, so I'm not due to see him until evening."

"So what are you worrying about? The guy is occupied all day and you can tell him exactly what's happening tomorrow night."

"I guess so," Chrissy said uncertainly. "It's just that with all these terrific-looking, friendly girls around, I can't be too careful. He might just walk off and never come back."

"And would that still be the worst thing in the world?" Caroline asked gently.

"How would you feel if Luke walked off and never came back?" Chrissy asked.

"You didn't answer my question," Caroline said firmly, "and I don't think you want to answer it because you're not sure of the answer anymore."

"I am sure," Chrissy said loudly. "And I'm really tired so I think I'm going to bed. Are you coming?"

"I'm going to stay out here just a while longer," Caroline answered. "Everything looks so beautiful tonight and the flowers smell so sweet—I just want to stand here and take it all in."

Chrissy rolled her eyes at her cousin's lovesick sap. "I'll see you later then," she said.

In bed a few minutes later, Chrissy found it impossible to go to sleep. Long after Caroline and Tracy were breathing easily on either side of her, she lay awake, her brain still in overdrive. Her sunburn had passed the major hurting stage and was now itching so that she wanted to wiggle her shoulder blades against the sheets constantly and could not find a comfortable position. But she knew it was not the sunburn that was keeping her awake.

That Ben, she thought, *Drat him and double drat him! Why did he have to show up now of all times? This was supposed to be the most romantic, wonderful vacation of my life—one that I would look back on when I was old and gray and tell my grandchildren about around the dinner table . . . and now Ben's here to spoil it! How can I relax and have a great time with Jeff knowing that Ben is on the same island?*

She turned over onto her stomach, burying her head between her arms. *I won't let him bug me,* she resolved. *I'll just pretend he's not even here and do exactly what I would have done with Jeff. After all, why should it bother me if he's shown up? Everything was over and finished between me and him long ago. I'm not the same girl I was when I left Danbury last summer, and I can't ever go back to being the Farmer's Wife of the Future! That's what Ben wants. I've just outgrown him,* she thought sadly. *But we sure did have great times together once. . . .*

Memories of a battered red pickup truck flashed into her mind—bouncing over rutted tracks to a spot beside the river where the willow trees grew . . . eating watermelon . . . laughing . . . playing hide and seek among the thick bushes on the bank until Ben found her in the hidden place and kissed her. Everyone teased them when they came back a whole hour later. . . . It had truly been wonderful once, but it was over, like part of her childhood. She had grown up and grown away. . . .

And Jeff is just as wonderful, she thought, trying to conjure up Jeff's tanned face, his short blond hair, and his piercing blue eyes that always seemed to be laughing. *I'll explain to Jeff about*

Ben tomorrow. I'm sure he'll understand that Ben is no threat—one look at those brand-new blue jeans he was wearing and it will be clear that he's not a threat!

She smiled to herself as she finally fell asleep.

Chapter 12

The next morning when they met Luke and Ben on the beach, Chrissy was reassured that Jeff would not see Ben as a rival or a threat. In fact, she thought, Jeff would probably feel sorry for Ben. The truth was that Luke and Ben stood out like sore thumbs on a beach full of tanned, fashionably dressed bodies. To begin with, they both had a real farmer's tan, extending up their arms only as far as shirt sleeves ended—and the rest of their bodies were still lily white. And instead of wearing the long, brilliantly colored swim trunks favored by the surfing kids on the beach, they wore plain old gym-type swim shorts.

Caroline didn't seem to notice that Luke looked funny at all. She flew across the sand toward him, flinging herself into his arms. He swept her off her feet and twirled her around until they both collapsed into the warm sand, laughing. Chrissy turned away to find Ben watching her wistfully. *How can Cara feel like that about a hick boy?* she thought angrily. *Doesn't she realize everyone is watching her?*

"Well, Chrissy, I'm sure looking forward to my first day on a real beach," Ben said. "Isn't this sand something?"

"You'd better put sunscreen on or you'll burn to a crisp," she replied, then felt guilty as she watched his face fall.

"There's some guy waving at you," Ben said, looking around with interest. "Is that Jeff?"

Chrissy looked up quickly. "Oh, no," she said with relief. "It's just some guys from California we met on the beach our first day here." She swallowed her embarrassment as Brett and his gang came down the beach with their boards to join them.

"You don't have to tell me," Brett said with a big grin. "These guys just got here!"

"That's astounding, Holmes," Tod chimed in. "How did you deduce that?"

"Elementary, my dear Watson," Brett said with an exaggerated English accent. "It was because they did not say aloha when we walked up!"

Everyone started laughing.

"I just can't get over that ocean," Ben remarked, turning to Luke, but his voice carried so that the whole group heard him. "I mean, look at the way those waves come rushing in all the time. You'd think pretty soon there would be no more water left in the middle and it would all be on the beaches."

More laughter. Chrissy could tell from the other guys' faces that they weren't completely sure whether Ben was joking or not.

"The actual water doesn't really move," Tracy explained. "It stays where it is and the waves are just like shock waves going through it."

"Is that so?" Ben asked, staring at the ocean, as if it might vanish. "I remember learning something about that in science class. Do you remember learning that, too, Luke? And now I'm actually seeing a real ocean!"

There was a stunned silence.

"This is the first time you've seen an ocean?" Jeremy asked.

"That's right. Our very first ocean."

"Where do you come from?" Tod asked, his voice hinting that the answer might be Mars.

"From Iowa," Ben said before Chrissy could stop him.

"How about that?" Brett said with interest. "I don't think I ever met anyone who actually came from Iowa before."

"Are the waves going to be small enough to give us another surfing lesson today?" Chrissy asked hastily before Ben could disclose that she was from Iowa, too. "I was doing pretty well when I got struck down with terminal sunburn."

"Sure, we can give you a lesson in a while," Tod

said. "The waves should get calmer around noon."

"I'd like to try that, too," Ben said. "Is there anywhere around here you can rent boards?"

"Sure, up there where the canoes are," Tod answered. "We'll give you some pointers if you like."

"Doesn't look too hard," Ben said. "But then I'm in football training. We have to be pretty good on our feet."

Why does he have to try and act so macho? Chrissy thought in disgust. *Who cares if he is Mr. Football Hero?*

"How long are you staying?" Brett asked. "If you really learn quickly, we can go over and ride the pipeline in a few days. These waves are too tame. We've been going over to the other side of the island every afternoon after the waves get tame here."

"Hey, that sounds pretty good. The pipeline—I like that," Ben said.

"Ben!" Chrissy warned. "Those waves get to be over twenty feet high!"

"What do you care?" Ben asked. "You don't have to come and watch."

He deliberately turned his back on her. "So, can you guys recommend fun things to do here?" he asked.

"You have to go dancing at the Tidal Wave," Tod said.

"And watch the hula show at the Banyan Court.

Those girls—wow, man—they make your eyes bulge right out of your head!"

"And you have to try a Mai Tai!" Brett suggested.

"What for?" Ben asked.

"Because it's good."

"But I never wear a tie," Ben said, confused.

The group erupted into noisy laughter again. Chrissy looked at Ben in embarrassment. How could he be such a hick? He didn't even seem to be embarrassed when he said things like that. *And weren't you the same when you first arrived in California?* a nagging voice asked within her head. *Didn't you keep making everyone laugh, and you were never sure what you had said that was so funny, so you laughed along?*

The group broke up then—the boys to catch the last of the good waves for the day, Ben to rent a surfboard, Caroline and Luke to wander into the ocean hand in hand, lost to the rest of the world.

"Are you coming swimming, too, or do you still have to stay out of the sun?" Tracy asked Chrissy.

"I guess I'll come in for a quick swim," Chrissy said. "Although I don't want to be anywhere near Ben when he gets that board. I have a funny feeling he'll be dangerous."

"He's certainly game, though, isn't he?" Tracy said with a giggle. "Ready to try anything once."

Chrissy rolled her eyes up to heaven. "He is so embarrassing, Tracy. I don't think I can survive a whole week with him around. He doesn't seem to realize he's acting like a geek!"

"It's only because everything is still so new to him," Tracy said as they headed down to the ocean. "I can still remember the first time you met a wave, Chrissy!"

Chrissy's cheeks flushed deeper red through her sunburn. She remembered that huge knock-out wave all too clearly. What a dodo she must have been! What a hick—and yet . . . all the people who had laughed at her had gone on to become her friends. Maybe she was judging Ben too harshly. Maybe she was only angry with him because she was really confused and angry at herself.

"After all," Tracy was saying, "the poor guy did fly halfway around the world to be with you again. There can't be too many boys who'd do that for a girl."

"I guess not," Chrissy said, poking her toe into the cool, clear water. "But what am I going to do with him, Tracy? I mean, look at him! The trouble is that I feel responsible for him. I can't just ignore him now that he's here, and I get the feeling that I'll need to keep him out of trouble. And what's Jeff going to say? Do you think he'll understand that Ben is only an ex-boyfriend?"

"I'm sure it will all work out," Tracy said. "Jeff doesn't have too much free time, does he? He's playing most evenings and sleeps all morning. That gives you plenty of time to keep Ben amused and still be with Jeff."

"Sounds wonderful," Chrissy said bitterly. "Just the sort of uncomplicated vacation I need right now."

"Don't knock it," Tracy said. "I wouldn't mind having two good-looking guys fighting over me."

"One good-looking guy at a time is fine with me," Chrissy said. "There's no way I can go back to Ben now. I wish he'd realized that before he came all the way out here."

"Chrissy! Hey, Chrissy!" She looked up as Ben yelled her name to see him running down the beach carrying an enormous surfboard.

"Ready to watch an expert in motion?" he called. He started to wade out into the waves.

"All you have to do is stand up on it, right?" he yelled, pulling himself powerfully onto the board and then rising unsteadily to his feet.

"See that? Nothing to it!"

"Ben, watch out!" Chrissy yelled as a big wave came up behind him. The next minute he had the board whipped out from under him and fell over backwards with a huge splash.

"You're supposed to ride the wave, not wait for it to tip you over," Chrissy said dryly as he swam an awkward freestyle stroke to retrieve his board.

"Like how?" he asked.

"Simple," she said, taking the board from him. "Lie on the board. Wait. When you see the right wave coming, start paddling. When you've picked up the wave, stand up." She demonstrated with a passing wave. To her surprise, the board was large enough to pick up the wave instantly and she rose to her feet before kneeling again, then jumping off sideways into the shallow water. "See?" she asked calmly, trying to act as if she were a surfing expert, not a lucky beginner.

"Yes, I see now," Ben said. He tried with the next wave and the next. One time he fell off to the right, then to the left. Several times the wave left him behind. At last he picked up the board and lifted it over his head. "I don't think there's much point in carrying on with this," he muttered. "I guess I'm just no good at it."

Then he waded from the ocean without looking back, leaving Chrissy with a strange lump in her throat.

Chapter 13

That evening Chrissy arrived at Jeff's apartment feeling more than a little confused. She still could not shake off the picture of Ben, walking up the beach with that surfboard, his shoulders slumped in a sign of defeat. She remembered him as he used to be at home—the star of the football games, doing his funny little dance in the end zone after a touchdown, walking with a swagger down the school halls the next day, and honking imperiously as he drove to pick her up in his truck. Had Ben lost his confidence because of her? She had been Ben's girl since eighth grade, and, even if she had moved on now, Ben had done nothing to deserve the way she had hurt him.

She kept imagining the rare football games

when Ben fumbled. The coach would bench him and say, "You're no good anymore, Hatcher. You just haven't got it anymore." But then the next game Ben would come back with a vengeance to play better than ever. He *never* gave up.

She also knew there was no way she could put him out of her mind during an evening with Jeff. *I'll just have to make him understand,* she thought. *He'll have to be patient for a few days. Just until I've settled things with Ben.*

She resolved to tell him all about Ben as she walked beside the canal to his condo that evening. *Maybe he'll even have some advice about how to let Ben down lightly without hurting his feelings too much,* she thought. *He is a guy, after all. He must know the right things to say.* She was feeling pretty confident as she rang the doorbell, but the moment she stepped into the living room, that confidence evaporated like a popped balloon.

She stood in the doorway and absorbed the scene. One lamp was turned on in the corner, throwing a mysterious pink glow over the rest of the room. The stereo was on softly, but not playing the lively rock of Jeff's band this time—it was playing a very old, slow number with lots of strings. And, to crown it all, there was a bottle of wine, two glasses, and a candle burning on the dining table.

"You like it?" Jeff asked, giving her a very special smile. "I figured your sunburn must have cleared up by now. . . ."

"Well, I don't know about that—it's still painful here and there," Chrissy said, trying to sound bright and confident. "Oh, my goodness—doesn't the room look charming tonight? You really did a good job on it. I'd no idea there was a sofa under all those socks!" She gave a high pitched laugh.

"Well, don't just stand there in the doorway. Come on in," Jeff said. "There's nobody around but us."

"There isn't?"

"My roommates are playing gigs tonight and they won't be back until way after midnight. So that gives us a whole lot of time together—just what we've been waiting for, right?"

"Oh, right," Chrissy mumbled.

"Glass of wine?" Jeff asked.

"You know I don't drink."

"Now's a good time to start. It's good stuff, Chrissy," he persuaded her. "Go on—just a little glass, after I went to all this trouble. . . ."

"Well, just a sip then," Chrissy said, not wanting to offend him. Her brain raced desperately as she watched him uncork the bottle and pour the wine. What should she do now? Her heart was beating quickly, and she felt lightheaded even without the wine.

"Here," Jeff said and handed her the glass. "To us—and to a great time in Hawaii, where the rest of the world cannot intrude."

"Funny you should say that," Chrissy said, putting on her bright voice again. "You'll never guess who I bumped into yesterday? My old boyfriend from back home."

"No kidding?" Jeff asked. "From Iowa? He came all the way from Iowa?"

"People do get out sometimes," she said. "It really isn't the end of the earth," she said with a self-conscious laugh.

"But it's still a long way," Jeff remarked. "Is he on vacation with his folks?"

"No, he's with a friend," she said.

"Oh, that's nice. New girl?"

"No, actually he's here with Caroline's old boyfriend, who instantly became Caroline's current boyfriend again."

"The one she talked about all the time in San Francisco?" he asked with a grin.

"That's the one. And now they are back together, gazing into each other's eyes like there's no tomorrow. It's sickening to watch."

"Don't you think two people should be in love like that?" he asked.

"Oh . . . er . . . sure. Of course I do."

"Good," he said, slipping a hand around her waist and pulling her skillfully toward him while balancing his glass in his other hand, "because you've got me right here and you can gaze into my eyes all you want. . . ."

His face was dangerously close to hers now, his eyes were holding hers in an electric stare. Chrissy could feel her heart pounding—half from fear and half from the excitement of being so close to Jeff. Slowly, deliberately, he brought his lips toward hers. They brushed Chrissy's lips teasingly, sending a shiver down her spine, then he crushed her against him, kissing her hungrily as he ran his hand through her long, loose hair. She was floating, high in a light, pink nothingness, not even conscious of breathing, when into this pink world a person in old-fashioned blue and white bathing trunks began to walk up a beach with a surfboard. She opened her eyes to find Jeff looking at her.

"Why are we still standing in the middle of the room like a couple of dummies?" he asked, kissing the tip of her nose. "Come and sit down." He pulled her toward the sofa.

You came here to talk things over, she reminded herself very firmly as she sat down.

"Now, what were we saying?" she chirped brightly. "Oh, I remember, about my ex-boyfriend and how amazing it was that he showed up here."

"Chrissy, let's not talk right now," Jeff said in a husky voice. His hand on her shoulder was beginning to pull down the strap of her sun dress. With his other hand he turned her chin toward him, beginning to kiss her again. His kisses felt so good—soft and exciting at the same time—but in the back of her mind she knew that tonight Jeff wasn't going to be satisfied with just kisses. She sat up, moving away from him.

"It's no use, Jeff. I have to talk to you."

"What about?" he asked grouchily.

"I've been trying to make light of it, but it's no

joke," she said. "You see, meeting Ben here has really confused me."

"You mean, you still think you're in love with this guy?"

"No, I don't think that. I'm sure I'm over him. But knowing he's right here on the island, that he came all this way just to see me . . . well, I'm confused, that's all."

"I don't understand," Jeff said impatiently. "Do you want me or do you want him?"

Chrissy sighed. "It's just not as simple as that. And I don't want him back. It's just that knowing he's here . . . well, it's made me uptight. I can't stop thinking about him. Even when we were kissing just now." *That sure sounded like a lame excuse,* she thought miserably. *Why didn't I just say right out that I just plain don't want to do it?*

"So what are you trying to say?" he asked bluntly.

"I guess I'm just trying to say I'd like a little time. That tonight's not right. I couldn't relax. Give me a couple of days while I sort things out with Ben and then I'll be back."

Jeff stared at her. "You want me to let you go around with this character for a few days to decide if you like him better than me?" he asked incredulously.

"No!" she blurted out. "You've got it wrong. You don't understand at all." The words came out in a rush. "I don't want to decide between you. I do want to be with you, Jeff. I came over here so that we could have time together, but Ben keeps

haunting me. I can't get him out of my mind—not because I'm in love with him still, but because he's here and he represents . . ." She took a deep breath. "I guess what I'm really trying to say is that I'm not ready for this!" She pointed at the candle, the dimmed lamp, and the stereo. "I really am only a little country girl at heart, Jeff. This just isn't like me. Ben's been like my conscience giving me a good hard shake." She turned toward him and put her hand on his shoulder. "Don't be too mad at me, please. I can easily see how a girl could get carried away by all this—carried away by you. You're a very sexy guy. But I don't feel right here. If I got carried away, I'd regret it all my life."

Jeff laughed and put his head into his hands. "Just my luck," he said. "I get the apartment to myself, all alone with a very cute girl and she turns me down!"

"Oh, it's nothing about you, Jeff," Chrissy said quickly. "You are the most wonderful, gorgeous guy I've ever met. I'm just asking you to understand where I'm coming from. I grew up with a traditional Midwestern upbringing. Why, do you know that back where I come from, people stand on the curb when the light says 'Don't Walk', even if there's no car in sight, and they wait to cross until the light says 'Walk', That's just the sort of people we are. Kind of boring, I expect you think, but we're all well behaved and we don't do anything illegal or immoral. It just goes against our nature, you see."

Jeff gave a big sigh. "I suppose I'll have to understand, won't I?" he asked. "You're not the sort of girl who's going to come around with a little friendly persuasion."

He started laughing then, though Chrissy couldn't see what was so funny. At least he wasn't mad, but even so, she decided that the kindest thing would be to leave right away.

Chrissy got up from the sofa. "Will I see you again?" she asked, trying to keep her voice even, realizing as she asked it that she might have changed things forever with Jeff and blown all her chances.

"I'm going to be kind of busy for the next few days," he said, not looking up at her. "I'll call you."

"Sure," Chrissy said. How everything could change in two seconds? Amazing how that incredible electricity between two people could be turned off as quickly as throwing a switch! She started to walk toward the door, but Jeff leaped up and grabbed her shoulders, spinning her around toward him.

"Oh, Chrissy! Why did tonight have to end like this?" he demanded, partially laughing in a tone of exasperation.

He stood, his hands on her shoulders, looking down at her, shaking his head. "I don't believe this!" he said with a huge sigh. "I really thought . . ." He managed a smile. "You are so delicious," he said, "I could eat you up!" He bent and nuzzled her neck.

All thoughts went out of Chrissy's head as a sharp pain shot through her. She let out a loud yell. "Ow, watch out for my sunburn. Ow, that's so sore!"

They both turned around as there was a scuffling sound at the window. Chrissy gasped as a figure leaped into the room.

"Get your hands off her, creep!" Ben shouted, crossing the room with giant strides.

Before Chrissy had time to react, Ben snatched Jeff away from her and knocked him to the floor with one smooth punch. Chrissy stared at both of them in horror.

"Ben, what are you doing?" she screamed at last.

"What does it look like I'm doing?" he asked. "I'm rescuing you. I saw this guy attack you, and I knew I had to save you. It looks like I stepped in just in time."

"He wasn't attacking me!"

"But I heard you scream. He'd gotten you in his arms."

"Ben, I screamed because he touched my sunburn," Chrissy said frostily. "It hurt, that's all."

Jeff sat up, rubbing his chin with a bemused expression on his face. "So this is the famous Ben I've heard so much about?" he asked.

"This is him all right," Chrissy said.

Jeff stared at Ben with an expression of disbelief on his face. "Do you normally go around busting into other people's apartments and knocking them over?" he asked. He turned to

Chrissy. "I thought you were just saying how you people back in the boonies were so law abiding and never did anything wrong."

"I did," Chrissy said, scowling at Ben. "I forgot to add that they can't resist meddling in other people's business!"

"I came to save you, girl. You should be glad you have a guy around who cares about you like that."

"For the last time—I did not need saving!"

"Not right this minute, maybe," Ben said, "but take a look at this place—the soft lights, the sweet music—this guy is a real con artist, Chrissy. You know what he had on his mind."

"Of course I know what he had on his mind!" Chrissy said angrily. "And it's nothing to do with you!"

Jeff got unsteadily to his feet, looked at Ben, and laughed. "If I'd known this was my competition, I wouldn't have worried too much," he said. "Well, golly, Miz Chrissy! I guess they don't grow brains too big back in the boonies!" He started to laugh again, but it was a harsh laugh this time.

"At least we know how to treat a girl right, back where I come from," Ben muttered. "None of this soft-lights-and-sweet-music routine to make her lose her head."

Jeff laughed even louder. "No, I guess you couldn't get quite the same romantic atmosphere in a cow shed," he said, "or is it a pigpen?"

"You're asking to be knocked down again, buster," Ben said.

Chrissy stepped between them. "Now just stop this, both of you. You're behaving like little kids, insulting each other like that. One more word and I'll knock you both to the floor—and don't think I couldn't, with one hand behind my back."

This made Ben chuckle and even elicited an honest grin from Jeff.

"She always did have a temper," Ben confided to Jeff. "You should have seen her push Tammy Laudenschlager into that heap of pies." He turned to Chrissy. "Come on, girl, I'm taking you home."

"You are doing no such thing," Chrissy said.

"I am too. Your folks asked me to keep a good eye on you and that's exactly what I'm doing."

"Just go, Chrissy," Jeff said. "We've already said what we've got to say, and I guess you two really deserve each other! I've learned something to-night—you can take the girl out of the boonies, but you can't take the boonies out of the girl. You'll always be little Chrissy from Iowa, won't you?"

"Yup, that's right," Chrissy said, looking at him steadily, "and I'm proud of it. Bye, Jeff. It was . . ." Chrissy paused now, suddenly feeling sad. It really was over with Jeff now—forever. "I had a great time with you. I'll always remember it."

Then she hurried out the front door before she could look at him again. Her feet clattered down the front steps and across the parking lot. She half ran, half walked without looking back. She could hear Ben's feet pounding on the sidewalk behind her, but she didn't stop or turn around. At last he caught up with her and grabbed her arm. "Chrissy, wait up. I can't keep up this pace in the heat!"

Chrissy did stop then, swiveling around to face him with such an angry expression on her face that he gave a half step backwards.

"Now, you listen to me, Ben Hatcher," she said fiercely. "I can take very good care of myself without your help. I do not need you to rescue me. Is that clear?"

"But, Chrissy, I only thought . . ." he muttered. "I did hear you scream after all. What was I to think?"

"You had no right to be following me in the first place," Chrissy said, "and if you had any sense in that head of yours, you'd know that I'm not the kind of girl who can be sweet-talked into anything she doesn't want to do."

She began to walk down the street again. He ran to keep in step with her. "Do you have to move so fast?" he asked.

"I'm a fast sort of person," she said. "I'm always going forward. You have to learn to move fast if you want to keep up with me."

He grabbed her arm, forcing her to a standstill. "Chrissy, I wish you'd stand and talk for a moment," he begged.

"We don't have anything to say right now."

"But that guy Jeff—did I understand right back in there? Did you and he just break up?"

"I guess that was what happened," Chrissy said.

"Because of me, right?"

"Wrong," Chrissy said firmly. "You had nothing to do with it, so don't go getting any ideas. We broke up because we didn't see eye to eye on certain important things—sort of the same reason that you and I broke up, too. I need a guy who can accept me as me, the way I am. Until I find one, I'm quite happy to do without. Good night, Ben." She started to walk again, then turned back. "And if I ever catch you following me around again—holy cow, will you ever be sorry!"

Chapter 14

By the time Chrissy let herself into the apartment, her anger had cooled off. She was sweating from the pace of her walk home and was suddenly exhausted. She could hear the hum of the TV set coming from the living room as she slipped through the empty hallway and into her bedroom. There was no way she felt like facing Tracy and her aunt and uncle right now. She wouldn't have the patience tonight to make polite conversation.

She walked across to the window and rested her elbows on the cold marble of the sill, peering out into the night and sniffing the sweet, heady scents of the garden. It must have rained during the evening because all the scents seemed to be magnified—the rich, earthy smell mingling with the sticky scent of the gardenia and the spicy fragrance of the ginger flowers. She stood there for a long while just breathing, not moving, not thinking.

She only turned around when she heard light footsteps come toward the door. She straightened up, expecting the footsteps to belong to Tracy. She was sure Caroline would still be out with Luke. But instead, Caroline came into the room, closing the door quietly behind her. She must not have noticed Chrissy in the darkness at first because she jumped when Chrissy spoke her name.

"Sorry if I scared you," Chrissy said.

"What are you doing here? I thought you were out with Jeff for the evening," Caroline said, coming over to the window and leaning out beside Chrissy.

"And I thought you were with Luke," Chrissy replied.

She heard Caroline give a dreamy sigh. "I was," Caroline said, "but Luke got a little sunburn so he wasn't feeling very well."

"That's too bad," Chrissy said. There was an uneasy silence between the two girls, then Chrissy said, "Doesn't everything smell good tonight? I was just standing here breathing in the air."

"Are you okay?" Caroline asked, putting a hand on her cousin's arm.

"I'm fine," Chrissy said. She corrected herself. "Well, sort of fine. I don't have a boyfriend anymore and I've just had a giant fight, but apart from that everything's just great."

"Chrissy, did Jeff come on too strong the way you thought he would?"

"Uh-huh." Chrissy nodded.

"And you had to fight him off and that turned into a big fight?"

"Not really."

"You didn't fight him off?" Caroline asked suspiciously. Then she checked herself. "I'm sorry. You don't have to answer that. What you do is up to you."

"I didn't have to fight him off," Chrissy said. "He was a perfect gentleman, almost. I convinced him with words, although I was all prepared for a quick wrestling toss!"

Caroline laughed. "So what was the fight about?"

"Ben."

"You told him about Ben?"

"I didn't have to say too much, since Ben was there all too clearly in the flesh."

"Ben went to Jeff's apartment?"

"He burst in to rescue me," Chrissy said dryly. Suddenly she laughed. "Oh, Cara, it was so embarrassing. You can't imagine—Jeff and I were just saying good-bye and Jeff touched my sunburn and I let out a yell because it hurt and Ben leaped in through the window! You should have seen him, Cara, like something out of an old movie. I mean, how ridiculous can you get? I nearly died. Then everybody shouted a lot and then I came home. Thrilling evening, huh?"

Caroline was laughing, too. "Sounds like the sort of thing that usually only happens in nightmares. Poor Ben. I'm sure he thought he was being the brave hero. It's rather sweet when you think about it. . . ."

"It most certainly is not!" Chrissy said, her anger returning. "Would you like to be shadowed for the rest of your life by your childhood sweetheart?"

Caroline shrugged her shoulders. "It shows that he really cares, doesn't it? You don't find too many people in the world who will do what Ben did."

"I know," Chrissy said, turning back to the window with a sigh. "I know he meant well, but how can I get it into his head that he can't win me back, Cara? I really bawled him out when we were alone together, but I still don't know if that did it."

"I imagine he'll get the message if you keep yelling at him long enough," Caroline said thoughtfully. "You are pretty frightening when you're angry."

"That's me, terrifying and cold," Chrissy said. She meant it as a joke, but the truth in it made her sad. She looked back at her cousin, her big eyes suddenly wide with anxiety. "Do you realize, Cara, that I've just gotten rid of two boyfriends in one evening? Is that dumb or what?"

"You told Jeff you didn't want to see him again, either?" Caroline asked.

"It sort of ended up that way," Chrissy said. "I got the impression that Jeff was not prepared to stick around just for my beautiful mind, if you see what I mean."

Caroline looked at Chrissy with concern. "Poor old you," she said. "I know how much you liked him. You must be hurting pretty badly."

"Not as badly as I thought I would," Chrissy said. "I guess coming to Hawaii opened my eyes about Jeff and about the way I feel about other things, too. I couldn't go on dating a guy, wondering all the time when I was going to have to fight him off again." She paused, drumming her fingers on the marble. "So now it's over. I am completely boyfriendless. How about that? But you know what? I don't really care. Being tied to one guy is for the birds. I am going to live from now on— parties, casual dates, a different boy twice a week, a long trail of broken hearts behind me. How does that sound?"

"Pretty impossible," Caroline said. "Knowing you, that is. You're an emotional person, Chrissy. I can't see you going for long without getting involved. I give you a couple of weeks before you fall head over heels in love again."

"No, thanks," Chrissy said. "I'll wait until I get back home. There isn't room in this place for two girls with silly smiles on their faces, floating around and sighing."

Caroline laughed nervously. "Is that what I do?"

"Absolutely. Oh, Luke—sigh, sigh. Oh, Cara—

sigh, sigh. It's disgusting! I suppose it will go on until you get married and live happily ever after."

Without warning, Caroline nestled her head into her hands and burst into tears. It was so unexpected that Chrissy just stood there staring at her for a long while. Finally she placed her hand gently on Caroline's back.

"Cara, what's wrong?" she asked. "Is something the matter between you and Luke? You didn't break up, did you?"

Caroline shook her head, still overcome with sobs.

"Then why are you crying? With happiness? Because if that's it, please stop being so happy—you are worrying me."

Caroline turned her head just enough to look at Chrissy. "I'm so scared, Chrissy," she said between sobs.

"Of Luke?" Chrissy asked. She still hadn't a clue what Cara was talking about.

Caroline shook her head. "No, he's so sweet—the sweetest guy in the world, in fact," she said, sniffling. "How could I be scared of him?"

"Of what then?" Chrissy asked in confusion.

"That it's all too wonderful and I'm going to go through all that terrible pain again when he leaves," Caroline said. "He is so optimistic about the future, Chrissy. He really believes we can work something out to suit both of us. He says he just won't let me go again, but . . ."

"But what?" Chrissy asked. "You're scared by that commitment?"

Caroline shook her head again. "I just don't believe it can work. It seems too good to be true. We'll be apart for our whole senior year and then we've got to find a college somewhere that we both like, and I don't think a college exists that won't be too hick for me and won't be too hip for him. I mean, you couldn't picture him at Berkeley, could you?"

"Your mom was at Berkeley," Chrissy reminded her cousin. "She was fresh from the farm in Iowa and she met your father there."

"That's right," Caroline agreed. "And she never went back to the farm again. But Luke will inherit his family's farm someday and the thought of living with two hundred pigs somehow doesn't appeal to me."

Chrissy laughed. "You've really been thinking that far ahead?" she asked. "Caroline, you are normally the practical, sensible one. You have one year left of high school, plus four years of college before you start thinking about pigs or not to pigs."

Caroline managed a weak smile. "I know you're right," she said, "and I know I'm getting upset over nothing. It's just that we were talking about the fact that he's going home in only four more days and that got me all depressed. It's like showing a kid a fabulous toy he's always wanted and then taking it away from him again."

"If I were you," Chrissy said, "I'd make the most of the four days. They have to keep you going for a whole year of calculus and physics and American government and AP English. Why don't you make them so wonderful that they will be etched in your mind forever, like a painting you can take out and look at whenever things go wrong?"

Caroline nodded slowly. "It's just that it's so hard to think of saying good-bye again."

"I know that," Chrissy said, "but if you really care about Luke, and I know you do, remember it will be just as hard for him to say good-bye. You don't want to make it even harder by creating a picture in his mind that's all mopey and dog face, do you?"

Caroline nodded. "You're right again."

"I'm always right," Chrissy said with a smug grin.

"No way," Caroline said, lifting herself from the windowsill. "What about the time you got me a blind date with the wrong boy and the time you fell into poison oak trying to take a short cut at camp and . . ."

"Shut up," Chrissy said, laughing. "One example would have been enough, not my entire life history of teeny-weeny mistakes."

"Teeny-weeny mistakes?" Caroline asked, beginning to laugh, too. "You call those things teeny-weeny mistakes? More like giant disasters!"

"Giant disasters then," Chrissy said. "And I guess you can add the scene with Ben leaping through the window to the list. In fact, my life seems to be a series of slap-stick comedies."

Caroline put an arm around her. "At least

people will laugh when they read that famous autobiography you're going to write," she said.

Chrissy slipped her arm around Caroline as well. "What a pair we are," she said. "Has there been a single week this whole year when one of us has not had some kind of crisis?"

"Maybe one," Caroline said thoughtfully. "That week in Disneyland, maybe. That's about it."

"Well, I've come to a decision," Chrissy said. "That emotional stuff is all over for me. No more getting involved, getting upset, breaking hearts, breaking my heart. I intend to use some of the skills I've learned during this past year. From now on I will be cool, sophisticated Christina Madden, the Snow Queen of the Midwest. . . ." She broke off, eyeing Caroline critically. "Are you crying again or do I detect a hint of laughter?" she asked in her cool, sophisticated voice. "I can't see what's funny about my future life as a jetsetting career woman. In fact, if you don't stop laughing, I'm going to start tickling you, and I happen to know exactly where you are most ticklish. . . ."

They were wrestling and laughing hysterically when Tracy and her aunt opened the door.

"Chrissy, Caroline, are you all right?" Tracy asked.

Chrissy and Caroline broke off in mid-tickle and looked up.

"We're fine, thank you," Chrissy said in her sophisticated voice. "We were just debating about whether I had turned into a sophisticated jet setter yet. Now, if you'll excuse us, I think I was winning the debate." She dove for Caroline's foot and began tickling ferociously as Caroline let out another shriek.

Chapter 15

For the next few days Chrissy threw herself enthusiastically into her new role as social butterfly of Waikiki Beach. She hung around with Tod and Brett and their group all the time on the beach, dragging Tracy with her and ignoring Ben when he showed up, too. Caroline was off with Luke most of the time in their own private world, and while Chrissy couldn't really blame her cousin, she was fed up with having sole responsibility for Ben.

Poor Ben still stuck out like a fish out of water. His back had burned as red as Chrissy's and he was confined to the shade, wearing a long-sleeved T-shirt most of the time. The only long-sleeved shirt he had brought with him proclaimed him King City 4-H Champion, which Tod and Brett found definitely uncool. In fact, teasing Ben had become one of their major occupations when they were not surfing. And to make matters worse, Ben believed everything they told him.

Once the boys told him that a long ribbon of seaweed was a poisonous sea snake and Chrissy laughed as hard as any of the others when he came flying out of the water after the seaweed had wrapped itself around his leg. And when a little voice nagged from the back of her mind that she was not being fair to Ben, she stifled it with a reminder that Ben was responsible for everything that had gone wrong on this trip and that he was even responsible for the end of her romance with Jeff. She had said this so many times to herself that she almost came to believe it was true. She wouldn't dare admit that Jeff would have dropped her even if Ben had not appeared through the window.

The one thing that was clear in her mind was that Ben had to learn a lesson. He had to learn that he was not allowed to interfere in her life and that his old-fashioned tactics were not going to work in getting her back. All the same, she couldn't help feeling sorry for him, and he was such a good sport about all the teasing that she secretly began to admire him, too—although why on earth he didn't make more of an effort to fit in was a mystery to her. She noticed that he never tried using a surfboard again and would only go into the ocean when he thought nobody was looking, splashing about with his ungainly freestyle at the edge with the little kids. But instead of encouraging him, Chrissy ignored him and concentrated on flirting with Tod and Brett.

One day Ben grabbed her arm as she walked in from the surf.

"Chrissy, what's with you lately?"

"Nothing's with me," she said coolly. "What do you mean?"

"I mean that you're acting like a big phony. You're acting like those snobby girls back home that you always said you couldn't stand."

"I am not a phony," Chrissy said. "It's just that I'm not the person I was back home. I've grown up and learned about the big world outside Danbury. I've just moved on, and you don't like it."

"And you do like it?" he asked.

"Of course I do. It's much more fun to be with the crowd, having a good time," she said, shaking the water out of her hair and turning to catch Brett's eye as he came in from the surf.

"I see," Ben said slowly. "And how do you think you're going to fit in, back in stupid, boring old Danbury when you finally decide to come home?"

"Maybe I just won't come back at all," she said, breaking away from his grip and striding back into the ocean, kicking up spray as she went. Angry thoughts spun around inside her head. *I am not being a phony. I am not being a phony,* she kept repeating to herself. *Why did he have to show up here and upset me? It's just not fair.*

"Hey, Chrissy," Tod said as she flopped down on her towel later. "We're having a beach party tonight, up at Queen's Surf. You coming?"

Chrissy had heard gossip about the wild beach parties that went on. She looked across at Tracy who was, as usual, reading a book in the shade, and then at Ben who was just sitting down beside them pretending not to listen. "Sure," she said. "I'd love to come to your beach party tonight. And Tracy will come, too, won't you, Tracy?"

"Mmmm?" Tracy asked, turning a page.

"We've just been invited to a party tonight," Chrissy said.

Tracy didn't say anything right then, but as they were walking home at the end of the day she spoke up.

"Why did you say we'd go to a party with them tonight?" she asked.

"Because it will be fun," Chrissy said. "Come on, Tracy, you've done nothing but lie in the sand and read since you've got here. You know that Jeremy likes you."

"But, Chrissy," Tracy said, worried frown lines appearing between her eyebrows, "let's not get carried away. These guys are fine to chat with on the beach, but we don't really know anything about them. You'd never think of going on a date with strangers at home, would you?"

"It's just a beach party, Tracy," Chrissy said. "Come on, where's your sense of adventure?"

"But we've heard about these parties," Tracy

said. "There's always beer and drugs and the police even raid some of them. My aunt would die if I got taken to jail."

"It won't be like that," Chrissy insisted. "These are nice guys, Tracy. We won't be in any danger. Please come with me."

Tracy sighed. "I guess so," she agreed, "but only because I don't want you going on your own. Besides, we'll have to be in by the ten o'clock curfew that my aunt set, and not too much can happen before ten, can it?"

"Of course it can't," Chrissy said. "Who knows? Perhaps you and Jeremy will really hit it off tonight. Then you can walk hand in hand in the moonlight with him."

As she said it she realized that she had not fulfilled her own dream of walking hand in hand along the beach with a handsome guy. *Maybe tonight,* she thought. *Tod's been flirting with me all week. Maybe tonight will be the night for me, too. . . .*

Tracy's aunt was not at all happy about the girls going to a party with people she didn't know. "You think because this is a relaxed island that bad things don't happen here," she said, wagging a warning finger, "but you have to watch out here, just like any other place. There are good people and bad people everywhere in the world. If you go, you two stick together and make sure you're home early."

"We'll be fine," Chrissy said. "I'm a tough farm

girl with muscles. Any guy who tries anything with us is going to be sorry."

"I'm sure you're both sensible girls and you'll come to no harm," Tracy's aunt said, "but don't get carried away with our warm tropical breezes!"

Chrissy laughed to Tracy as they walked toward the beach. "I don't know what your aunt thinks we're going to do," she said. "I just want to dance and talk and have a good time. I'm certainly not going to this party looking for trouble."

The party was already in full swing by the time they walked down the steps and onto the sand at Queen's Surf, a park area at the end of Waikiki Beach lined with palm trees. Someone had made a bonfire and a group of some twenty kids was gathered around it. One or two people were attempting to dance in the soft sand while others were slouched against a stone wall beyond the fire. A tape player was blasting out heavy rock.

"Oh, hi, Chrissy. Hey, Tracy," Brett called, waving to them. "Grab a beer and come on over."

"No beer, thanks," Chrissy said. "Do you have a soft drink?"

Brett laughed. "Didn't they repeal prohibition in Iowa yet?" he asked. "I'd have thought you'd have wised up after a year in civilization. Nobody here is going to check your ID you know."

Before Chrissy could say any more, Tod appeared, thrusting two beer cans at Chrissy and Tracy. Then he moved on without giving them a chance to protest. They stood there, taking polite sips as the others milled around them. The crowd seemed to be growing all the time and soon it became obvious to Chrissy and Tracy that some of the party-goers were already very drunk. Two guys lurched up to Chrissy.

"Don't I know you from somewhere?" the first one asked, peering into her face.

"I don't think so," Chrissy said. "Maybe you've seen me on the beach."

The boy laughed. "I don't hit the beach in daylight, babe," he said. "It must have been from another life." He peered even more earnestly. "Were you around in Roman times? I was a charioteer, you know. What were you?"

"A goddess," Chrissy said quickly, bringing a laugh from other bystanders.

"I know who she is," the second boy joined in. "She's Vanna White. Doesn't she look like Vanna White? Hey, Vanna, I wanna buy a vowel. Give me an A . . ."

Tracy pulled Chrissy's arm. "I don't see Jeremy here. I didn't think he'd show up, somehow."

"He'll show up," Chrissy whispered. "It's early yet."

"I get a funny feeling he won't," Tracy said. "It's not his thing."

Chrissy nudged her with her beer can. "Come on, Tracy, loosen up," she said. "We're here to have fun, remember?"

"But I'm not having fun. Are you?" she whispered. "Let's go home."

"It's fine," Chrissy whispered. "They're harmless. You don't need to worry."

She turned back to the group of boys and waved her arm. "Three A's," she said sweetly. "Now, do you want to solve the puzzle or spin again?"

This is just dumb nonsense, harmless fun, she kept telling herself. *I'm having a great time here. This is fun.* But it was as if she had to keep winding herself up to go along with the bright and bubbly image.

Tracy stayed as close as Chrissy's shadow until Jeremy finally showed up. Chrissy smiled her approval as Jeremy took Tracy's hand and led her away from the crowd. Then Brett dragged Chrissy off to dance and Tod joined her for a crazy French can-can. Tracy reappeared at her side as they flung themselves into the sand at the end of the number, giggling.

"I don't want to sound like an old kill joy, but Jeremy and I are ready to leave," she said. "Do you want to come with us?"

Brett was tugging at Chrissy's hand again, urging her to get up for another dance. "No, you two go have a good time," Chrissy answered. "I'll be fine here."

"Are you sure?" Tracy asked, watching with concern as Brett began to dance with Chrissy. "I don't like to leave you like this."

"Do I look like I'm in danger?" Chrissy asked, laughing. "Everything's fine. I'll just dance a while longer, then I'll come on home. You know I can't resist dancing. Hey, Brett, twitch your arms like this! Let's all do the Chicken!"

"Well, I guess I'll see you later, then," Tracy yelled above the loud noise of the music.

"Okay, Tracy. See you later," Chrissy called back, then threw herself wholeheartedly into the dance.

When it ended someone else asked her to dance, and then someone else again. Finally she was exhausted.

"I have to stop for a while," she told the big Hawaiian guy she was dancing with. "My feet won't move anymore in this soft sand. I need to sit down, okay?"

"Okay with me," he said. He walked with Chrissy out of the center of the group and pulled her down beside him on the sand. "In fact, it's fine with me, baby," he whispered. "I like this a whole lot better than dancing."

"Hey, wait a minute," Chrissy said as he put his huge hands on her shoulders. "You've got the wrong idea, buster. I just wanted to sit down."

"So did I, baby," he said and laughed. "But now that we're sitting, let's make the most of it."

She tried to wriggle free, but his hands tightened on her shoulders, forcing her backwards into the sand. She looked around wildly, trying to catch a glimpse of Brett or Tod or any of the other guys she knew, but they all seemed to have disappeared. The entire beach seemed full of strangers. As they swayed to the wild beat of the music, their bodies lit up red with firelight, reminding Chrissy of an Indian war dance she had seen once in a movie. The dancing was no longer exciting—it was frightening.

"Hey, cut it out," Chrissy said, attempting to joke. "I don't even know you."

The big guy laughed. She could see his white teeth flashing in the firelight. "Sorry about that. I'm Joey and you're Chrissy, right? Now we know each other." He forced her back onto the sand, kissing her clumsily. She struggled to free herself but it was like trying to move a stone statue.

"Leave me alone, creep," she managed to shout, breaking free of him. "Let go of me right now or I'll scream for help."

That made him laugh even more loudly. "Scream away, baby. Who's going to hear you over all this noise? Besides, the guys around here know better than to interfere between me and a girl. I get real mean if anyone disturbs me."

The huge hand held her down again.

Anger was now mingling with fear inside Chrissy. She realized for the first time that she was completely alone in a situation she could not handle. Until this moment she had always felt confident that she could deal with any boy who got difficult.

"If you don't let me get up this instant, you'll be sorry," she threatened. "I'm not some weak and wimpy little girl. I wrestle hogs on a farm, you know."

Joey was shaking with laughter. "That's great, baby. I just love a good wrestle," he said.

"You asked for it," she threatened, swinging out her arm and trying to force his arm behind his back. But as she tried to force him away from her, she realized that her famous muscles were sorely out of shape and certainly no match for Joey. He moved easily, taking her two hands into one of his and pinning them to the ground above her head.

"Now," he asked. "What was that you were saying?"

"Help!" Chrissy cried out, wriggling desperately. "Somebody help me!"

It's hopeless, she thought. *Nobody will come. Nobody can hear me.* Sand was getting in her face as she thrashed her head around, making her cough and choke. She could hardly breathe from the weight of Joey's body leaning on her. *Please don't hurt me,* she pleaded silently.

Then miraculously, she spotted somebody standing over them. A hand reached down and grabbed Joey's thick hair, wrenching his head backwards.

"Get off her, buddy," a voice growled.

"Mind your own business and let go of me or you'll be sorry," Joey snarled back.

A hand slid around his throat. He started coughing, then turned and sprang to his feet. "You'll be sorry," he said again.

"I don't think so," said the calm voice in the darkness. "You'll be the one who's sorry if you don't get out of here right now. That's my girl you're messing with."

"Ben?" Chrissy asked incredulously. She staggered to her feet, shaking the sand from her hair as she moved.

"Just get out of the way, honey," Ben said calmly, "while I show this creep why I'm the boxing champ of Danbury." He turned to face Joey. "You ready to fight?"

"Forget it," Joey growled. "You take her if you want her. I already got a record for fighting. I don't want to wind up in jail." And he melted into the crowd.

Chrissy and Ben stood facing each other.

"Are you okay?" he asked.

She nodded.

"You're not going to start yelling at me for interfering again, are you?"

Chrissy flung herself into his arms. "Oh, Ben," she cried, tears welling up and spilling over. "You saved me. I was so scared."

He held her close, stroking her hair, and whispering soothing words in her ear.

At last she stopped shaking and looked up at him in amazement.

"It's like a miracle. You showed up at just the right moment. How did you know? Did you hear my prayers or something?"

"Heck no," he said with a grin. "I've been here all evening."

"You have?" she asked, her temper beginning to rise again. "You just sat there, watching me and didn't do anything until just now?"

"How was I to know whether you wanted to be

rescued or not?" he asked, stepping back as her eyes began to take on that familiar angry glint. "I mean, heck, Chrissy, you might have been enjoying it for all I could tell."

"Enjoying it? Ben Hatcher, have you flipped your lid? That great big oaf just grabbed me. I was only dancing with him—I didn't flirt or anything. Why would you think I'd want him to paw me like that?"

Ben shrugged his broad shoulders. "I don't know," he said hesitantly. "I just thought that now you'd become all citified and that, you'd be more broad-minded about things like . . . you know."

"Is that what you think of me?" she asked, feeling both angry and upset. "You think I've become loose?"

He shrugged his shoulders again. "You kept on telling me that you'd changed and outgrown me and that you could take care of yourself. I was just following your orders not to butt in."

Chrissy looked up at Ben. He held her gaze steadily.

"You're right," she said. "I did tell you all those things, but they weren't true. I knew that all along. That's what I'd been telling Jeff that night at his condo when you did your Tarzan act."

"Telling him what?" Ben asked quietly.

"That I couldn't change the way I was—the way I'd been brought up. I didn't tell you that before because . . . because I didn't want you to think you'd won a point over me."

A slow smile spread over Ben's face. "I see," he said.

"And don't go getting any wrong ideas, Ben Hatcher," she said quickly. "Just because I'm very grateful you showed up to rescue me does not mean I'm ready to come leaping back into your arms."

He stood there, nodding thoughtfully. "I understand that, Chrissy. You might be the same person deep down, but you have changed in lots of ways. I know we'll need time to adjust to each other, but I'm prepared to stick around. I'll just keep plodding along behind you—good old Ben—and I'll always be there when you need me. How does that sound for now?"

Chrissy reached out and wrapped her arms around his neck in a big, friendly hug. "That sounds just great," she said.

He slipped an arm around her waist and kissed the top of her head. "Come on, girl," he said. "I'll walk you home."

Chapter 16

The day before Luke and Ben had to leave for Iowa, Chrissy, Caroline, Tracy, and Jeremy threw a good-bye picnic for them on the other side of the island. Jeremy and Tracy had become friends and he offered to drive them all in the car he had rented. Chrissy was happy for Tracy. Not that she could see Tracy's relationship with Jeremy blossoming into a great romance or anything—every time Chrissy tried to talk to them, they were always discussing literature or chemistry. Chrissy didn't think that was a very promising start of a love affair, but at least they were good friends.

It was nice to see Tracy animated and lively again and to know that she had fully recovered from her long bout with mono. The only problem for Chrissy was that, with everyone paired off, she was left alone with Ben. She was still very confused about her feelings for him.

"The trouble is," she had told Caroline the evening before, "that I'm too comfortable with him. He's like an old shoe that fits me well and won't give me blisters."

Caroline laughed. "That's flattering," she said. "I'm sure he'd like to hear what you think of him."

"I don't mean it in a bad way," Chrissy said hurriedly. "What I'm trying to say is that part of me wants to go back to being his girlfriend again. But another part of me wonders if I only want to get back with him because it's the easiest and safest thing to do. Remember how we discussed whether guys gave us goosebumps or not? Well, I don't get goosebumps when I think of Ben."

"You got them with Jeff, but that didn't make him right for you, did it?" Caroline pointed out.

"I know," Chrissy said. "Perhaps I want too much. I want goosebumps and security, too. Is that impossible?"

"I don't think so," Caroline said. "You feel secure with Ben. That's the best way to start, isn't it? Just relax, Chrissy. Let things happen."

Chrissy looked at her cousin in amazement. "I never thought I'd hear *that* coming from you! Is this the same Caroline I met last year who made out a list every time she went shopping, who had her binder organized two weeks before school started, and who started studying for finals right after spring break?"

Caroline shook her head. "You still exaggerate," she said. "And I'm still the wonderful, organized person you met back then. It's just that I've learned not to plan personal relationships because plans never go the way you want them. You have to leave a lot to fate."

"I'll try," Chrissy said with a grin.

Jeremy parked the car beside an almost deserted beach screened from the road by large banyans and palms.

Up until today Chrissy would have said that she preferred beaches like Waikiki, full of tanned surfers, hot dog stands, and music, but somehow this quiet beach was just right for today: a narrow crescent of sand with a clear lagoon, and waves breaking on the reef beyond it. Chrissy grabbed the Frisbee and tossed it to Caroline.

"Here, catch," she said.

Ben leapt up to intercept. "Boys against girls!" he yelled back. "Luke!"

"No way," Chrissy yelled. She tackled Ben and tried to drag him down into the sand. What started off as harmless Frisbee throwing soon turned into an all-out Frisbee-football game between all six of them, and they didn't stop until everybody was covered in sand, exhausted and laughing helplessly.

"I didn't know beaches could be so much fun," Tracy said, splashing the sand out of her face with sea water.

"We country boys know how to enjoy ourselves, don't we, Ben?" Luke commented, smiling. "Cara, keep still, you've got sand on your eyelashes."

Chrissy watched as Luke tenderly removed the sand. It looked like he was picking it off one grain at a time. She could see him looking at Caroline as if she were the only thing that mattered to him in the world. Chrissy suddenly felt jealous that Caroline was the one who had found Mr. Right. When she finally looked up, Ben was staring at her.

"You want to go swimming?" she asked brightly, jumping up.

"Sure," he said, getting up to follow her.

"You should try the masks and flippers," Tracy said. "The sea life is just fabulous here."

"Good idea," Chrissy said. She handed Ben a snorkel and mask and slipped a pair on herself. Then she sat in the shallows, easing her feet into the flippers.

"Come on, slowpoke," she called to Ben. Ben had sat down on the sand to put his flippers on. "Don't put them on until you're in the water!" she warned.

"Why not?" He stood up and tried to walk toward the water's edge. "Hey, how do you make these things work?" he yelled. "My feet won't go forward."

Chrissy started to laugh. "You look like you're starring in 'The Invasion of the Frog Man'!" she said. "I said to wait, because the flippers are so hard to walk in. Turn around and walk backward."

Ben did this until he was standing beside Chrissy in the water.

"Okay, now put on your mask," Chrissy said. "You put the snorkel in your mouth like this and slip the mask over your head . . ."

She demonstrated with her own, the way she had learned at summer camp. "Great, let's go!" She slid gracefully into the water and began to move forward with smooth, easy kicks, her hands by her sides.

"How come you're suddenly the water expert?" he growled. "Back home you could hardly doggy-paddle across the pool."

"So I learned a thing or two in California," Chrissy said. "Come on, it's not hard. And the fish you'll see are just fantastic."

But Ben was already pulling off his mask. "I don't think I feel like swimming right now," he said. "I shouldn't get the sun on my back—it might get burned again." He walked out of the water, still wearing the flippers, and taking giant frog steps. After he took them off he walked down the beach and sat on the rocks at the far end.

"Oh rats," she muttered, standing up and pulling off her mask. "Why does that boy have to keep ruining my life?"

She pulled off the fins and flung them up on the beach. Ben was staring out at the ocean, his blond hair blowing in the wind.

"Now listen here, Ben Hatcher," Chrissy said, making him reel back with surprise at the force of her words. "You and I have to get some things straightened out if we ever want things to work between us."

"What's gotten into *you*?" he asked, eyeing her suspiciously.

"Nothing's gotten into me," she said. "It's what's gotten into you—all this macho stuff!"

"What are you talking about?" he asked.

"I'm talking about snorkeling just now. And why you wouldn't go with me."

"I told you, I didn't feel like swimming."

"Nonsense, Ben. You wouldn't go because I could do it better than you. This is the twentieth century, Ben. Girls are better than boys at some things. And they are now allowed to succeed, in case you didn't know."

Ben looked away. "Nobody said you weren't allowed to succeed, Chrissy."

"You never said it, but you thought it. It's the way people think back in Danbury. Boys are football heros, girls are cheerleaders. Boys take shop, girls take home ec. Men work and their wives stay home. That's the traditional way, isn't it?"

"I guess it is," Ben said.

"Well, it's not right for me, Ben," Chrissy said. "I want to be my own person. I don't want people to turn to my husband and say, 'and is this the little woman?' the way they do to my mom."

"Do you want them to turn to you and say 'Is this the little man?'" Ben asked, grinning suddenly.

Chrissy had to smile. "I don't want to dominate, Ben," she explained. "I just want to be free to do what I want to—free to try new things, and free to make mistakes. I guess that's what I've learned in California. I've tried a lot of new things there. Some of them I've failed at, but I've learned something from each of them and that's what's important."

"I don't want to tie you down, Chrissy," Ben said quietly. "I never did." He turned and looked at her with such longing that she felt tears well up in her eyes. He reached out and took her hand. "Do you think we could try again, Chrissy?" he asked. "We've got senior year ahead and it's not going to mean a hill of beans unless I'm going to the senior prom with you."

"I guess we could try," Chrissy said slowly. "Just as long as you don't get angry if I can do a few things better than you."

"Okay. As long as you don't beat me out for my place on the football team," he said.

Chrissy giggled. "Don't worry."

His hand tightened on hers. "I will try, Chrissy," he said. "Let's go for a walk, okay?"

Slowly they walked together along the shore. The sun was setting on the other side of the island and the sky was pearl gray.

"It's hard to believe that this time tomorrow I'll be back in Iowa," Ben said. "I bet I'll be wondering if this was all a dream."

Chrissy nodded as she kicked the shallow water.

"Do you think you'll miss me a tiny bit when I've gone?" he asked.

"Of course I'll miss you," Chrissy said lightly. "Who else is going to entertain me by breaking in through windows, falling off surfboards, and walking down the beach like a giant frog?"

"I see," he said quietly. He looked down at her with his serious, little-boy eyes, his hair still flopping, as it always did, across his forehead.

Chrissy reached up and touched the tip of his nose. "Why do you look so upset every time I tease you?" she said. "We've always kidded around, haven't we? Now you seem to take it personally."

"Because now I'm not sure of you any more. You can only tease people you're sure of," he said. "You're not the same person I knew a year ago."

"Underneath I am, Ben," she said. "I kidded myself for a while. I thought I'd changed and become one of those sophisticated girls I admired in school. But I haven't changed one bit. I'm still the same sweet, adorable Chrissy you once knew! The same Chrissy who makes dumb mistakes, speaks when she ought to keep her mouth shut and believes all the things her Mom taught her back home in Iowa. And I will miss you, Ben."

"Oh Chrissy," he said, shaking his head and laughing at the same time. "You know what?" he asked, his hands tightening around her waist.

"No—what?"

"You do talk too much, always did," he said. He pulled her toward him, kissing her firmly on the lips.

They stood there for a long time, not moving, the water lapping at their ankles, the light fading as the sun sank behind the mountains. Suddenly Chrissy broke free, pushing away from Ben with a loud yell. "Yahoo—look at that!" She turned and started to run down the beach to where Caroline and Luke were sitting. "Cara! Look at my arms! I've got goosebumps!"

Chrissy looked back at Ben, who was watching her with a bewildered grin on his face. Somehow, she and Ben belonged together—but they had had to travel all the way to Hawaii to find that out. Chrissy knew it was crazy, but in the middle of the beautiful Hawaiian sunset, all she could think about was going home to Danbury, Iowa. Because now she knew someone very special would be waiting for her.

Here's a sneak preview of *Double Take*, book number nine in the continuing SUGAR & SPICE series from Ivy Books.

"Oh no," Chrissy shrieked, flinging her hands over her ears. "Don't tell me! Something horrible has happened, I know it. I just knew everything was too good to be true!" She threw herself across the bed.

Caroline turned to her mother. "Mom, it's not Aunt Ingrid, is it? Or the boys or Uncle . . ."

"They're all okay," Caroline's mother assured her.

"Then . . . what?"

"A tornado," Mrs. Kirby said simply. "Chrissy's family's house—it's gone. There's nothing left. Nothing at all."

ABOUT THE AUTHOR

Janet Quin-Harkin is the author of more than thirty books for young adults, including the best-selling *Ten-Boy Summer* and *On Our Own*, its sequel series. Ms. Quin-Harkin lives just outside of San Francisco with her husband, three teenage daughters, and one son.